The Look of Things

Mystery of the Haunted Library

June Seas

CAROLINGIAN
PRESS

Contents

Ideas, like ghosts ... must be spoken to a little before they will explain themselves ...

—Charles Dickens, *Dealings with the Firm of Dombey and Son*

Chapter 1

Bad Weather

A ll night a wind such as they had never heard before roared around the house. It didn't come in gusts, it maintained a steady roar, driving branches and buckets and boards from the west. Well, it did gust sometimes in an even louder scream, and just when you thought it was all over because the screaming seemed quiet, you listened, and heard the wind's permanent throbbing, like a very long train passing but never past. Sometimes there were crashes when things were slammed at the house.

The great wind had perhaps alarmed the dog, and now Dog just had to get up and go downstairs. Sue considered. The glowing "Big Ben" alarm clock said it was just barely one a.m. "No, Dog, it's not time yet, not for a long time." Dog tried to settle but turned around again and pushed her nose next to Sue's face, staring into the dark at her. Dog often attempted to communicate silently with her, willing her to read Dog's mind.

Her dog was a watchdog. By this, Sue meant that Dog had an unerring sense of time. Whenever the family needed to measure time, whether it was 20 minutes to cook rice or time for someone to arrive at home, Dog was like a timer, and would whine an alert at precisely the correct time to turn off the stove, or welcome a visitor or whatever. So now Sue wondered if maybe Dog had some other sixth sense and was so insistent for a reason—maybe the wind was about to crash something through the window, maybe Sue should obey. She picked up the dog and crept downstairs in the dark. She froze at the foot of the stairs, startled when the motion-detector spotlight at the house across the way blared directly through the window at them.

The deer set it off all the time. She looked back at the stairs where—no doubt it was just the porch light beams, fractured into pieces through the mosaic glass of the door's window? A spiral made of daggers of light quivered midway up the stairs. A dark spot in the center swayed.

Well, that was just her shadow of course?

She turned away rather than dwell on that scary thing on the stairs. She looked through the front window quickly at and then away from the miserable blue eye of the porch spotlight across the road, and took Dog out the back door. She wasn't dressed but who would see, at night? The wind made it difficult even to breathe and the sticks flying by and banging into the cars were scary. Dog struggled back up the stoop. Sue grabbed her afghan and curled up with Dog in the plump feather sofa, dutifully watching and listening to the wind, until they both slept.

***

The next morning was bright, but the wind continued to roar, sounding like the sea which never stopped rolling. Across the way a large white bag flew by and then it was impaled on the trees, corners caught like arms outstretched. The thing danced just like a cartoon ghost. Sue watched the ghost, fascinated. Finally the ghost freed itself and crept along the ground like a white animal, circling a few times, curling up and breathing. It would periodically heave and struggle.

Wait, was some creature caught in the bag? Sue sat up and strained to see, but the white thing then tumbled away down the far side of the hill.

A white carton was left behind on the hill, unmoving. Sue hadn't noticed that before, nor seen it arrive. She would look when she took Dog out.

Good thing there's no school, since I am just a slow puddle of thoughts today. Sue ticked off in her head what if anything she had to do today—nothing yet, the rest of the house slept, including Dog. Maybe she would go to the library. She got herself some cereal.

When she walked out with Dog, the white box was nowhere to be seen. There were just masses of dead pink earthworms stranded on the sidewalk. A black empty garbage bag floated from a tree branch high in the sky, like a Halloween monster decoration. Sue shivered with a sudden chill, and hurried Dog along, running up the steps to find her mother making coffee. Ma and the kitchen felt cozy and smelled good. They hugged and chatted.

Sue's mother disagreed with the library plan, however. "No, I think it's too windy to go out today. Too dangerous. You can't walk to the library today." The kitchen door rattled and shuddered.

Her father was chasing down their trash cans from the road. Her mother wasn't dressed yet, or maybe she was. Ma didn't brush her own hair or dress properly on days off, which seemed like it would be wrong and uncivilized, but maybe it wasn't really; her mother just pretended they lived in a log cabin in some camp settlement somewhere and the only thing that mattered was tending the family and the livestock, which she could do in her flannels and boots with no socks. This wasn't very different from her brother staying in his superhero costume on Saturdays. On days off, they pretended there was no one outside to see them.

The wind whined steadily and louder. "Listen! It sounds like a train. What if that is a tornado? Just stay downstairs today. The weather warning will expire after noon. Then maybe I'll drop you at the library." Sue knew they didn't have tornadoes in their part of the country; still, she had also heard that the sound of a train and a green sky could mean a tornado. The sky looked normal, though.

Chapter 2
Locked Out

By the afternoon it was just a normally windy day. Their mother drove Sue and her sister Joella to the library, to make sure there were no downed wires or other hazards, and in case any trees were still falling down. The few blocks between their house and library seemed to be clear, so Sue and Joella got the ok to walk home when they were through. The library was in some kind of cell phone satellite dead zone, so there was no service for touching base once there, you had to make arrangements before you arrived. Anyway Sue and Joella were not allowed to have phones yet. In emergencies, kids were allowed to call home from the front desk.

It was very unlike Sue's mother that she didn't wait to make sure they got inside the library before driving away; but this time, as the result of some unknown distraction, when they turned around on the library porch and waved at her, she just waved, looked into her mirrors and pulled off.

Sue felt a moment of panic when she pulled at the big wooden door and it didn't budge. Not even a fraction, like it would have bumped just a little and relapsed, if it were locked.

"They must be closed? Maybe because of the storm?" Joella searched the front windows for a paper taped up, THE SEMBLANCE PUBLIC LIBRARY IS CLOSED FOR INCLEMENT WEATHER, but there was none. (Sue always liked to think of the word "inclement" to describe people she met, or some days she got through: "lacking in clemency, or mercy".) The chandelier appeared to be lit, but the front desk chair seemed, temporarily at least, vacant.

They both banged on the door. Sometimes the library door unexpectedly locked during business hours, and someone had to get up and let the patron in, or, sometimes the door would already be open minutes before opening time, when the library staff thought it was locked, and you would walk in, and the staff would look up, blinking uncertainly. Then throughout the day you would see them getting up and jiggling the doorknob, testing the lock, puzzled.

The two girls ran back down the porch steps and stopped to look up at the windows.

"Hey. I never even noticed that third chimney before? Look at that, in the middle of the roof? right in the front?" The library was like a little old house. Well it was a big old house. Sometimes it felt little because each charming wing upon wing had been added over centuries, until the rooms were stacked in different directions atop multiple staircases. The girls had had a class trip to the library as every primary grade had done, for the local history unit; the many fireplaces were pointed out, and the names and histories of the occupants through the years recounted. They had examined the seam in the brick showing the different ages of the additions, and counted the fireplaces, but neither remembered this black metallic funnel rising from the roof, smack between the dormer windows.

At that moment the wind suddenly blew sharply, out of nowhere, and they resolved to try the back door. As they turned the corner a huge gust of wind knocked Joella back into Sue and both fell onto the sidewalk, seats first.

"Ouch! What are you doing?"

"I didn't do anything! The wind is really picking up again! I hope the back door is open!" Hair whipping into their eyes, they scrambled up, headed into the wind and stomped for emphasis up the ramp to the back door.

"Cool, look at the slugs!" There were dozens of the slimy creatures crawling up the ramp and over the banister railings toward the door, leaving string trails of goo marking their courses. Joella crouched and peered at them. "I wish we could look up at them and see their faces, instead of looking down at their little tentacles. They can see us, you know."

Ugh. Sue waited and checked the sky. She didn't understand why some kids studied everything under their feet but never looked up at the clouds; a fast moving, huge dark one was now approaching on the wind. "Slugs don't have faces like the ones in picture books, you know. I don't think."

Joella jumped up and pulled at the door this time. "It's locked!" There were no windows on this wall. The girls looked at each other. Sue tried too, for yucks, and fell back startled as the door opened out in her hand. Both girls stepped in quickly, giggling nervously. The wind took the door from Sue and banged it wide, then slammed it shut with a boom.

The library seemed quiet, as it often was of course. The lights were on. There was a skunky smell, but that was not unusual, either. (There was said to be a skunk in the garden, which came for the bread an old woman tossed there for the birds–unless the skunk came to eat the birds? Or the old woman, to feed the skunk?)

The chair was pushed away from the circulation desk as if one of the library staff had just got up and headed into the stacks. Joella had to go to the bathroom, and Sue went into the youth room.

A new woman perched in the chair at Ms. Kaycee's librarian desk. She was small and old, in the sense that she could be a mother or a grandmother or a great-grand. Sue could never tell ages of grownups, but the lady seemed older than the pretty mothers and fathers who came to the library with little toddlers, old enough to be Ms. Kaycee's mother. The woman popped up from her chair. She wore a long black flowy jacket, open to show a patterned blouse, and black sneaker-ish shoes. Her pants were once black but faded, and so loose like a dress that you couldn't really see any legs in them. The woman's eyes were opened very round and wide as if she were staring in shock.

On the desk was a large white box.

Chapter 3

Locked In

"Isn't the wind so wonderful, after all the rain we had; it will certainly take all that wind to dry up all that mud. We always seem to get just what we need, don't we?" The woman continued to stare at Sue. Sue noticed the little woman was wearing a jeweled insect on her lapel. It appeared to be a fly but perhaps it meant to be a bee? Ms. Wanda, the little chalkboard sign said.

"Hi, are you Ms. Wanda? Where's Ms. Kaycee?" Sue noted the pattern on the blouse appeared to be flies and wasps. She watched the box, which looked like the one she had seen on the sidewalk at home, but how could she be sure, really.

"Ms. Kaycee had to leave to take care of a family member in her country. I am sure we all miss her very much. How can I help you today?" The spot in which Sue stood before the librarian's desk suddenly stunk like cigarette smoking. Sue coughed and moved away.

"I'm okay, thanks." Sue slipped between the shelves to browse, pulled down another mystery and went to the reading room.

She climbed into a little cushioned seat built into the window frame. The book was open in her lap but she stared out the window for a while instead. They were only a few blocks from the beach, and the garden outside the window consisted of yellow pebbles on top of sand, and giant ceramic pots of pungent summer flowers and herbs. She watched small birds hopping in the garden and the haze of bugs round the pots; had the wind died down again? Then she watched, fascinated, as one soaring shadow traveled darkly over the ground. It was funny how sometimes you would see only a shadow, if you were looking, and not the predator itself, a hawk or gull. It was funny how you look down so much to see where you are going, you see only the shadows. We rarely squint up into the sun to see the thing itself looming over us.

Sue started at the sound of a book thumping onto the floor. She got up and looked at a book which seemed to have fallen off a shelf—a thick adult biography of someone she didn't know. She peeked between the rows of bookshelves, but no one else seemed to be in the room. She picked up the book and placed it firmly on the top shelf of the empty re-shelving cart.

"Hey!" Jacky, Angelica, Hanna and Joella tumbled into seats around a table. Joella was littler but liked to follow the big kids even better than following Sue.

"Hey."

"Did you just get here? We've been here all day. We came early for the movie. Somehow Jacky knew what we were thinking and showed up, too." Everyone grinned. "All the families with little kids left after an hour so we had the Club Room to ourselves. I saw Ninja Princess before but the power is out at home, so ..."

"Ms. Kaycee put out good snacks today, too!" Jacky chimed in.

"Well you would know, Jacky, I'm sure I didn't get any."

Angelica and Jacky had a weird way of talking to the group while looking only at each other. Jacky would steal stuff from Angelica until she chased him and grabbed his hands to get it back, and sometimes Angelica would say teasing things just a little mean to him, but if either of them went about their own business and ignored the other, they were both miserable. Now they both smiled at each other too long, until Sue said, "You mean Ms. Wanda. Ms. Kaycee's gone."

"Oh, we didn't see who, we came into the movie late when it was dark," Jacky blushed, "and grabbed seats. " Jacky and Angelica looked at each other.

Hanna asked what about this Ms. Wanda, and what do you mean Ms. Kaycee is gone.

Just then Joella, who had been sitting under the table with a book, clambered out. "Sue, I want to go home now. Did you get your books yet?" Joella dragged over a backpack stuffed with books. This week she was studying an assortment of animals from Australia, most of which were killers. She loved the little shiver, the frisson, she experienced when reading about exotic dangers from the comfort of her little bed.

"Did you want this one? I think it fell out of your backpack." Suddenly the very Ms. Wanda appeared behind Joella, holding out a book with a picture of a snake slithering right toward the camera.

"Oh, okay, thank you." Joella took the book from Ms. Wanda without looking up, and knelt on the ground to stuff it into her sack.

"My name is Ms. Wanda. I am the new youth librarian. I think I know your names. You must be Jacky, and Angelica and Hanna, and of course I've had little chats with Joella and Sue."

Now Sue knew the adage not to judge a book by its cover, and she heartily believed in it. She especially believed in it because there was a popular new standard of faith making the rounds: trust the "vibes" you get, not a person's words. Energy doesn't lie. People posted this a lot and Sue was afraid sometimes they were talking about her, that they had decided they didn't like her "vibes" and didn't believe her sincerity when she tried to be nice. Maybe they thought she gave off bad vibes for reading during lunch. Maybe they misinterpreted her shyness or nearsightedness for haughtiness. Maybe her vibes seemed different.

Sue was trying to place in her mind Ms. Wanda's fragrance. When she talked, if you were too close, she smelled sort of like decay. Rust? Or rot?

But there were lots of perfectly legitimate reasons for old people to seem funny sometimes, and Sue really didn't want to know about the details. So Sue would give Ms. Wanda a fair chance. The youth librarian was often the one person in the library who thought about a kid's feelings. In Sue's experience, people at the library might mean well, but they were innocently mean. Inclement. They chatted with the parents they knew, and cooed over the little babies, but they were sticklers for rules. It didn't occur to them not to raise their voices, publicly announcing your name and checkout history when you had overdue fines, and embarrass a kid when your card was expired, and they wanted your parents to come in with proof of their address and that their property taxes were paid. Most of her friends' parents weren't very comfortable communicating in English and worked until after the library closed; the kids walked or biked to the library as a safe place to stay until their parents got home. Patrons were proud to show their proof of identity, but pained at being asked for it; they thought their right to be in the country was being challenged. But rules are rules.

Sue's father always said, "rules are tools." Her parents were lawyers, and the whole family enjoyed debating a kid's foul-up of the house rules, and what was the purpose of the rule, and the history of what had occasioned the rule, and whether it properly applied to this instance, and if it did, if it should be changed, amended. Which made Sue think about being given an opportunity to make amends, and clemency. Amen.

Sue hoped Ms. Wanda would be the understanding kind of person. She hoped she would remember what kinds of books they liked best, and would let them use the pencils and crayons on her desk. Sue hoped she wouldn't just say, "rules are rules", as a conversation ender. Sue would give her a chance to be likable, if she was Ms. Kaycee's replacement. If she was just a substitute, well, then she was just as ordinarily strange as subs usually were. You could stand anything for a little while.

But now it was almost closing time. "Bye-bye! See you again soon!" Ms. Wanda stared after them as the group of kids said bye and loped down the hall to the exit.

"She's different." Joella dropped her sack again and knelt to tie her shoe. "Did you see her eyebrows?"

Sue, who had a history of difficulty correcting her eyesight, sometimes missed such details out of habit. Because she didn't used to be able to see such things clearly, she had stopped noticing. She usually just had some idea of the whole picture.

"They were like, wiggly gray things sticking up at the corners, like, like an owl or something." Jacky stepped over Joella and pushed at the door. Which refused to budge.

"Oh, the door was sticky coming in, too." Joella jumped up to help as Sue threw her shoulder into the attempt to push open the door.

Hanna ran down the hall, shouting, "Ms. Wanda! Can you let us out, the door is locked?"

She returned cockily leading Ms. Wanda into the foyer. Between the sparkling chandelier and the threadbare rug, Ms. Wanda looked even smaller and paler, and her eyes were really round and staring now. It was true, there were crooked white hairs sticking up out of each eyebrow, though maybe it was because her eyes were opened so wide. The staircase railings behind her looked like a cage from which she was just tentatively emerging.

Ms. Wanda put both tiny wrinkly hands against the door. "I'm sorry, but I can't seem to open it.

"Don't you have a key?"

"Well, of course I have a key! But it isn't locked. You see, even if it were locked, the door opens from the inside anyway, to let people out. So no one could be accidentally locked in ..."

Ms. Wanda showed them the button lock. Turned vertically or horizontally, nothing changed. The door would not open.

Joella sat down and started crying. "I miss Georgie and Shea!" Georgie was the little superhero brother. Shea was Dog's real name, but they called her Dog because she was more likely to answer to that. Sue looked worried. Jacky and Angelica raced each other to the back door, with the same result.

"The storm must have caused the doors to swell. We won't be able to get a carpenter in until the morning. We will just have to make a night of it. Won't this be fun?" Ms. Wanda looked grim, so they could not tell how she meant it.

Hanna put her hands on her hips. "My mother will be worried." They all nodded, then jumped, as the old windows on either side of the door rattled and something crashed upstairs. The lights went out.

Chapter 4
Lights Out

J acky cursed, and then joined Angelica and Hanna in
screams of laughter. Joella threw her arms around Sue
and sobbed dramatically. Sue bent down and whispered
into her ear, unwrapped Joella from her legs and took her
hand instead.

Now closing time on a Saturday was well before
dark, and the walls having been raised a century before
electricity, there was plenty of dim light available from
the many slits of windows. It would be quite a while until
anyone at home started to worry. Ms. Wanda toddled to
the front desk phone. "No phone service." She banged
down the phone with what looked like triumph.

"We could call the police?"

"No phone service!"

"Hey, let's pull the fire alarm!" Jacky seemed to have a good idea where there was a fire alarm. Ms. Wanda stopped him.

Hanna said, "Great, then we will be locked into a very loud, noisy library. We already know we have to get out, we don't need an alarm to tell us that. "

Angelica stood for a moment wondering. "Is anyone else even in here?"

"What was that crash anyway, did the roof cave in?"

Ms. Wanda appeared to be rooted to the spot at the front desk, blinking.

"I'm on it," and Jacky started up the dark steps, two at a time.

"I'll come with you." Angelica raced him. Hanna, Joella and Sue followed, rather than be alone with Ms. Wanda—probably for no reason other than that kids always tended to herd together rather than be left with an awkward grownup.

It appeared the roof had not fallen in. The top of the stairs was dark, but there was enough light coming from the windows in the front room to see. This front room was a poetry reading room, with more books on shelves, and the longest table ever, and one of the many bricked up fireplaces. Children were generally discouraged from using the upstairs room. There were several doors labeled

"Staff Only", one in the poetry room, and one at the other end of the hall, from where the crashing sound had come.

Of course they checked the poetry reading room first. There was light there, and being well behaved children and library cardholders, they were not usually inclined to open doors prohibiting public admittance. Nothing appeared out of order, though it felt very strange with the lights out. On the few times any of them had been up there, it always felt kind of like a holiday: shiny old brass things on the mantel, sparkling chandeliers over the polished and gleaming wooden table, red wool patterned carpet; it looked like your family was about to set the table for a feast. Now in the dark it still had a feeling of anticipation, but a nervous one, as you might if you were hiding.

They looked at the Staff Only door. Was it a closet or a room?

Anyway the sound had come from the other side of the hallway. And that far Staff Only door seemed like it must be a room; why would there be a hallway all that way only to get to a closet? Plus, though the hallway was dim, cold daylight came out from under that door, which meant windows.

After whispered discussion, they all resolved to check the Staff Only door at the end of the hall, to see what had crashed; except Joella, who refused, and had climbed into a corner chair to watch out the window for any news from outside.

Sue followed Hanna, Angelica and Jacky. She hadn't realized it was so very many steps. How long could this hallway really be?

Jacky entered through the door prohibited to the public, and immediately yelled and backed out, slamming the door.

"What was it?"

"I'm not going in there!" Jacky crouched in a little nook outside the Staff Only door. Now that they were here at the end of the hallway, they could dimly see that he sat on the bottom step of a staircase which went up curving to nowhere, ending in a wall.

Sue pondered this staircase silently, as Angelica slowly opened the Staff Only door and peeked around. "It's just a mannequin." They all hesitantly entered, even Jacky. Inside was a dressmaker's headless model, with an old dress on it, in the middle of a storage room with aisles of shelves and boxes. Large square white hat-sized boxes were haphazardly stacked in a tall sculpture behind the dress model. The room didn't appear particularly dusty, and it was likely used regularly by library staff to rotate the seasonal exhibits. There was yet another sealed door in the far wall, but stuff was stacked in front of it.

Old photos in convex frames were on the floor leaning against the wall, wedding photos and soldier photos and photos of fire engine companies. There were neat stacks of varicolored papers, and boxes of paint brushes and pencils. There was a pile of rugs, one of fur, on top. It was not readily apparent what had made the crashing noise.

"Ew." Sue thought Hanna was remarking on the fur but she was looking down at the bottom of her shoe, and examining the floor. "I think I stepped in glitter glue." It was the only mess on an otherwise polished floor, except for a snaggle of twisted yarn. The glue wasn't dry, still sticky, and the yarn lay partly in the sticky puddle.

Then Angelica noticed that the yarn trailed off across the room. "It's pretty, actually." Angelica picked up the yarn and tugged, but couldn't pull it in from the skein or wherever it ended.

The sound of a child's crying began behind them. Sue started. "I'm coming, Joella!" and they all followed Sue back down the long hallway, without looking back at the stairway to nowhere, and without even closing the door.

Chapter 5

The Winding

J oella was sitting on the floor in front of the fireplace. "I heard Georgie in the chimney! He was crying!" Joella looked wildly at Sue.

"Joella, Georgie is home with mom and dad. You probably heard your own echoes, or a bird on the roof or something." Joella remained on the hearth, whimpering.

Hanna stood by the window reading a tall thin book she had pulled off the shelf. "Hey, this is kind of weird. Why would there be a book of nursery rhymes up here, instead of with the poetry in the children's room? I never heard of any of these. Here's one, do you know it?"

The book's cover was all over text in faded brights, "A Victorian Baby's Book". Hanna traced with her finger the illustration of a ball of yarn unrolling, and then read:

The Winding

Sticks, bricks, iron and bone.
    Mud, rock, sand and foam.
    Leaves rattle, snows fall.
    Hide behind the chimney wall.

    Look within, look without,
    Close your eyes and turn about.
    Inch by inch, going home,
    Turn and twist, gift or loan.

    Mud, rock, sand and foam,
    Sticks, bricks, iron and bone.
    —Traditional

"Hanna, I don't know. It sounds kind of familiar, it reminds me of something. What should we do now?" A remote hiccup in the sobbing of a child sounded dimly from the chimney, and stopped. Joella had stopped crying and was staring at them, listening. Just then, the chandelier blared on, and one of the tiny bulbs exploded and tinkled down over the table. Angelica gave a little scream. Then they heard each step on the hallway stairs creak in succession.

The five children, (not counting the one Joella had heard in the chimney, though the chimney was silent, too), stood frozen, staring at the door. But the steps stopped. No one came in at the door, or made any further progress up or down the stairs.

These steps just creaked in turn that way sometimes, they knew. No Ms. Wanda appeared. They listened, to see if they could hear anything downstairs, but with thick old plaster walls, there was no hearing sounds below.

"Well the power is back on. Do you think we can get out now, or call someone?" Hanna was more than ready for the next step toward resolution of this adventure.

"I'm for opening that door. What if there is a lost child up here?" Angelica pointed at the Staff Only Door.

"Actually," Jacky said, "I happen to know what's in there, just a little kitchen, some snacks on a shelf, water and soda in the refrigerator, and a janitor closet, I think."

The others narrowed their eyes at him and he looked at Angelica sheepishly.

"But I'll check it out, to make sure."

"What kind of snacks? The food will come in handy if we are stuck here." Hanna was all for it and headed for the door knob.

"Shouldn't we ask Ms. Wanda first?" Sue was doubtful about taking anything from a Staff Only door. Jacky rushed past Hanna, threw open the door and the two of them went through.

When the rest of them squeezed in, Jacky and Hanna were gone.

Angelica flipped on the light switch and said, "Jacky, come out of the closet." She strode bravely to the second door in the kitchen. Joella was looking up and down the shelves to see if there were any treats she liked there. Jacky, Angelica and Hanna had probably just eaten them all at the movie. Sue stepped behind Angelica to peer over her shoulder while she opened the door.

It wasn't a closet.

Chapter 6

Ghost Town

The door was very heavy, and it took two hands to push it open. Icy air blasted into the kitchenette, and the girls looked down at a flight of steps which turned after a landing. There was natural daylight coming in from a frosted skylight. The stairs seemed brand new, compared with the historic parts of the building.

Angelica offered to hold the door, for Sue to venture down the staircase just a little ways until she could see around the bend. "So it doesn't close, sticking you out there, and so we can see and hear you." Sue groaned, but agreed to take just a few steps down. Joella was now behind Angelica, peering under her arm at Sue.

Sue called out, "There are two doors down here. I don't know which way Jacky and Hanna might have gone. But this door is an Emergency Exit! Then there are more stairs down to a door with a sign which says, 'Keep this Door Closed at all Times'. "

Suddenly Angelica and Joella clambered down the stairs to the landing to stand with Sue as the door behind them banged closed. "Someone was coming! The door to the kitchen was opening, so we slipped through down here and closed the door! Shh!"

The girls crept down to the cellar door and made themselves small under the stair, where there were soiled brooms and a rusting shovel leaning against the brick wall. The children were quiet for as long as they could be, listening. No one seemed to come down after them. There were some creaks in the floor overhead, some running water, and then silence.

"Do you think Jacky and Hanna went out the exit and just left us here?"

"The risk of opening the exit door is that it will set off some kind of alarm. That's always what the sign says; do you think it will?" Sue never opened those doors, but she would if there were a fire of course.

"I say we try it. If the alarm goes off, we have to just run. If Jacky and Hanna aren't home already, we will have to get our folks to come back to the library with us to check that other basement door, to see if we can find them."

Joella complained that she had left her books downstairs. The other downstairs.

"Joella. We'll come back for them tomorrow."

"But my summer homework is in there!"

"Tomorrow." Sue had a way of adopting their mom's "firm" voice, which was really irritating sometimes. But Joella was glad she was with Sue, and she took her hand and clutched tightly.

Angelica took a deep breath, pushed open the door the tiniest bit, and winced. No alarm yet. She plunged outside and stopped. Sue and Joella were right behind Angelica.

Jacky and Hanna were there on the sidewalk.

"Thanks a lot, guys. We were so worried about you. Why didn't you come back for us? You just left us there!" Angelica punched Jacky on the arm.

"No, we didn't! We found this exit and tried it, and then the door locked and we couldn't get back in! We were trying to decide what to do next!"

"Let's go home. What a day. Bye, guys." Hanna waved to Sue, turned and was already headed for the corner, and Angelica followed with Jacky in tow.

Sue had to stop and think which way was home, on her mental map. They had never used this exit door before, or knew it existed, so outside the door was a new perspective. This door opened into an alley side street; one could turn left toward Main, or right, to a corner with the street which ran a block past the library's rear neighbors. Those neighboring buildings backed onto the library garden, and the cross road, parallel to Main, was a block further past their route home. Nevertheless, rather than having to walk past the front desk windows of the library, Sue just felt better turning right, and heading right around the block and then towards home.

As they turned onto the street, Sue realized this route would be uphill a long way and then a long curving drop to the little one way street which would lead to her own neighborhood. But they were sort of committed already. Sue and Joella trudged up Bank Street.

There were no lights apparent in any of the houses, though it was still daylight; so it was hard to tell if the power was out up there, or the residents weren't at home, or if they just didn't turn on electric lights in the daytime. Sue thought of it as "up there", because the houses were not on the street, exactly. The rear of the library's gated garden was bordered by a stone retaining wall taller than a man, and a ramshackle weedy hill sat atop that wall; on top of that hill, piled the old houses.

They had not walked here before. This street had a weird smell, like an infection. The tree branches met in the middle over the narrow street, so that it was like walking through a green tunnel. There was furniture on the porches of the houses, high up over their heads, but the houses and street seemed empty of people. A few old cars and trucks were parked nose to tail on the other side of the street, but none of them looked like they'd been used lately. They were kind of dusty looking. The whole street looked like a ghost town.

Chapter 7

Weird

J oella was tired and watching her feet slap on the sidewalk. She started to emphasize the slapping of her rubber toe capped sneakers on the concrete, and laughed as the sound sharply echoed off the stone walls.

A pale dark girl rose up over the wall on the hill. Joella stopped short and looked up. Sue said, "Hi," and tried to keep walking, dragging Joella.

"Hello," the girl put her hands on her hips. "Where are you from?"

Sue and Joella stopped and turned back a little. Sue recognized the girl as an older student from school. The girl was typically a little aloof at school, and she was neither avoided nor bullied because she seemed confident in not caring what anyone thought. But you couldn't call her popular because she did not court anyone's attention, and she tended to travel alone, or tolerated a group walking in the same direction. She was called Rowan, Sue thought. She gave the appearance of being tall, but if you stopped to think, she actually took up very little space.

Sue bumbled out, "From school. I mean, we are coming from the library, and headed home. But I think you know us from school. I mean, you might not know me, but I've seen you at school." Sue blushed. The girl looked at her impassively.

Joella blurted out, "We have had a terrible day at the library!"

"Oh, dear! I wonder why?" The girl held up her hand and peered into a jar she was holding. "Well. Why don't you come up into the garden, and tell me about it?" She pointed to some rough steps made of dirt and logs which climbed around through a break in the rock wall. Joella smiled and looked up at Sue for approval. Sue was overcome by curiosity and a sense of adventure in getting to know a new and potentially advantageous school friend. The two girls climbed the steps.

"Rowan," the girl confirmed, hurling her name over her shoulder as she led them through a little iron gate to a tiny patio under a tree next to the house. Sue and Joella gave their names and Rowan responded by telling the names of all the little ferns and flowers which grew in pots or in the ground around the patio. The patio surrounded a tree stump just the size and height of a stool to sit upon, and Joella was about to jump up onto it.

"Leave that! That's the story stump. It's sacred."

Joella jumped up and down in place, instead. "Is that a frog in your jar?" Joella had been itching to see it.

"I would not keep an animal in a jar! This," holding up the little jar, "is hypericum—St. John's Wort. And jasper, with veins of quartz. I like these, don't you? I was collecting when I heard you banging along on the sidewalk." She set the jar on a little table at the center of three unmatched chairs, and Sue and Joella peered into it. The color of the glass was a teal blue and the sun glinted off it. The contents were concealed until you looked in at the top.

Sue was a confident science student and she took the jar in hand and held it up to eye level, then unscrewed the top and looked in, getting a grassy, earthy whiff. There were black berries on a stick with some leaves still, dotted with holes; and a stone which she wanted to touch, but was too polite to dump it out into her hand, and too shy to ask permission. The stone was a rough chunk of spotted rusty red, laced with white crystal lines. Sue returned the jar to the table. "How do you know their names?"

"Oh, we make a study of it. Herbalism, plants for healing; and the properties of minerals." There was a mug of tea on the table, and Rowan offered, "I was just having that tea, I'll get you some."

Sue and Joella responded simultaneously, talking over each other.

"No thanks—"

"With sugar?"

Rowan said, "OK, come on," and went through an old wooden and screen door. The girls followed her in. Even though the metal screen meshing and the damp wood surrounding it was so dark and blackened, the entire door was so light you could push it open with just a finger. It closed with a light and friendly bounce, so unlike the battle the girls had with every exit from their own home's automatically closing steel door; that one was hard to open and hard to close, but when it finally did, it bit one's ankles.

But though the door at home was unfriendly, their Dog was not, and never nipped or tripped them. Shea was the little welcome rug at the door who would jump up smiling and wagging and healing the door's injuries. Here, a cat, or something, leapt away from them into the shadows.

"Guests, Acantha," Rowan called out to the something. "Make yourselves at home, ladies." Rowan opened her arms palms up in the direction of a round table with three chairs shaped differently one from the next. She crumbled a clump of dried tea into a tiny pot, poured hot water over it from a kettle on the stove, and reached up to take two more mugs from a shelf. Sue and Joella sat at the table. They watched these adult-like behaviors with some awe, though truly they could each feed themselves; still they were not in the habit of serving their peers in the same manner, since mom or dad handled the hosting.

Sue wanted very much to ask if anyone else was home, but she considered it might sound rude. Rowan seemed to hear her thoughts though and replied, "Mum's home, but she only comes out at night."

A chill breeze puffed into the kitchen, and the screen door bumped open and shut with a click. Sue noticed the screen was patched in places with little squares, diamonds, of meshing, stitched onto the screen on the diagonal. The little squares interrupted the moire pattern of light shimmering through. The side of the screen sagged open a little where it needed further mending.

"Feels like autumn is here early." Rowan put the mugs on the table. Without a word she went to the door and slung a patterned woven blanket over a rod mounted above the door. The thick curtain cut the light but also made it warmer. She pushed two mugs over and gave them each a spoon on a clean napkin folded just so, and pointed to a jar in the center among an assortment of tiny bottles and shakers on a rotating platter, a Lazy Susan. The little teapot was under a child's shrunken wool hat with a tassel on top. Rowan lifted this tea cozy off and poured out their mugs of tea. She pointed, "Honey."

Joella sat up on her knees and reached for the honey pot.

"So what happened at the library? Do you need help of any kind?"

Sue was startled at the directness of the offer piled upon the polite question. "Well. Nothing bad actually happened to us or anything. It was just a weird day. Which is not that unusual at the library, if you know the place." Sue had been reflecting more about the happenings on the way home.

Joella nodded, adding, "People seem weird until you get to know them." Rowan watched them and sipped.

Sue asked if the lights had gone out on the street. Rowan looked surprised. "Oh, I don't know?" Sue looked around for a clock or something but couldn't see one.

Sue continued, "Anyway the electric went out but finally came back on. There's a new librarian. The doors were sticky and we couldn't get in, and then we couldn't get out. We heard noises but couldn't find out who made them. We left through the emergency exit!" It didn't sound so strange when you told what happened instead of what it felt like.

Rowan smiled. "Well, I don't know if I believe in 'strange' so much. Isn't everything? Weird? How can you tell the difference." Rowan wore a tee shirt with a giant leaf of some kind on it, over a long rippling dress, and she was barefoot. Her hair was very long and dark and hung unevenly, you couldn't really say where the edge of it stopped. She sat up very straight on her backless chair and held her head very high. She seemed much bigger and older. And no weirder than their own mother on a day off. But definitely stranger than the kids at school. Strange in her equanimity. "But I am sorry you felt scared. Scary things are only fun if you choose them, and if you know you yourself are truly safe. You probably did not plan on being scared at the library."

Sue thought about Joella's fun with poisonous animal books, and about the storm last night which started everything. "Thank you for having us. We should really go home."

"I'm glad we have become friends. Come by again," Rowan said. Sue felt giddily lighter. The door bounced cheerfully behind them.

The shadow creature slipped out of the house after them, and may have followed them home.

Chapter 8

The Freep

Sue and Joella race-walked the rest of the way home. Of course Sue's strides were longer than Joella's; but in a walking race, she limited herself to a quicker, shorter stride, so that the girls remained neck and neck, to maintain the suspense of the race. They wound down the street and when they arrived in town, Joella skipped ahead to the traffic light post and pressed the button for a "walk" signal. "I won!"

It was dinner time but still light outside. Their house was on a shady little one-way street across from a so-called park. The park consisted of the sidewalk through a few trees, and a grassy area sloping down to the canal. It was really just a small flood plain. An iron park bench defined it as a park. A person in a dark hooded cape and holding a staff was sitting on the bench at the bottom of the hill, facing the canal. The girls did not remark on this, since there was usually someone there, someone who had nowhere to go.

The girls clattered up onto their porch. Oddly, the front door was locked. If anyone had been home waiting for them, the front door would have been open.

"Oh, I can't believe they are not home! Of all days," Joella complained. "And I am so hungry." They peered in through the window, leaving their fingerprints and nose prints all over the glass, and then with one thought ran around to the side door. As expected, it was open and they went in and bolted it behind them.

Sue hated the side door because once inside you could go one way down to the cellar and one way up to the kitchen door, and she didn't like to look at the dark hole of the cellar on her right, when there were no lights on down there. She quickly ran up the six steps, brushing past the flannel shirts and hoodies hanging on the wall hooks, to the kitchen where she spun and waited for Joella to dramatically climb the steps, sighing heavily. Then she shut the kitchen door behind Joella. Dog jumped between them on the cool, clean floor, smiling and waggling.

They looked for the note on the table. It said:

We are out. Georgie had a small accident, he is fine but he needs a few stitches. We are at hospital with him.

Don't worry. Have frozen pizza for dinner. Be home soon, XO

"Oh no, I knew it! I heard Georgie crying!" Joella screamed and hid her face behind her hands.

Sue picked up Dog for a cuddle. "Mom says he's fine and don't worry. And you couldn't have heard Georgie. Let's just do this. I am so tired."

Joella beat her to the freezer, took out the frozen pizza and put some in the toaster oven. Sue poured water into two glasses. She looked in the fridge for a while and then took out a bag of lettuce salad, and arranged some on two plates for them. The girls then tumbled onto the sofa and ate in front of the TV. They had been watching a science fiction series about a family stranded somewhere in the universe on a strange planet with a robot, and there was a funny new episode each time featuring one of the kids. This one wasn't about the little brother, so that was good, but really, he always came out of it okay.

The phone rang and Sue had to race Joella and push her away to grab it.

It wasn't Mom. Sue shook her head at Joella and mouthed, "Hanna". Sue spoke into the phone. "Hey!...My brother hurt himself somehow and is at the hospital with my parents...No, he's okay...We are just watching TV...Yeah, ok, that's a good idea. See you soon."

Sue hung up. "Hanna and Angelica want to come over for a meeting."

Joella rolled her eyes and returned to the television. Sue thought about their visit at Rowan's. She scanned the cabinets to see what she could offer her guests later. They weren't allowed to use the stove when they were home alone, or knives; and her friends had probably eaten dinner already. She rummaged for a fruity herbal tea bag, dropped it in a pitcher with some warm water, and left it in front of the window. She could call it "sun tea" and pour it over ice.

Sue opened the front door and looked out. The hooded figure was still out there on the bench. Hanna and Angelica were walking down the street toward her and waved. She went to pour the tea.

"Aw, did you get a cat? She's so shy!" Angelica crouched, trying to see under the porch swing.

"What? No." Sue came out and bent over and the shadow animal streaked out off the side of the porch.

"Don't touch it! A feral cat might be sick," Hanna lectured, and marched into Sue's house. Angelica and Sue followed her in and the girls each stooped to greet Shea the Dog, then gathered around the counter in the kitchen.

"We need to make a plan," Angelica announced.

"A plan for—?" Sue poured out the tea.

"Oh, your mom's not home, you don't know!"

"Know what?" Joella came over to the counter.

"School's not starting!"

Hanna informed them that the Semblance Public School District had called all the parents, and school was going to be out indefinitely. The early fall break would continue until further notice, but would hopefully start within a few weeks. The storm had caused major damage to the school building, its roof was caved in and there had been an explosion of some kind. The whole street had been evacuated.

Semblance Central School sat at the end of a road. A few homes lined either side until the end where the playing fields and playground were, and then the circular parking lot and school building. There was no other way but in, on that street, so it was a nice quiet street; they had always felt pretty safe from drive-by predators.

"So what's the plan?" Angelica pressed.

"What?"

"How are we going to see Ja—people? What about our town history projects that will be coming due? What about our magazine that we were starting? What about Book Club?"

Book Club was really just Sue and one other student, Harry, but they followed Rules of Order for each meeting, and took it very seriously. They met in the school library during Club Period after classes biweekly. Maybe, someday, someone else would join; it really was very fun. Angelica knew about it because sometimes she and Jacky stopped by for the snack; they didn't ever read the book. And Joella always stayed after with her for the Club but did her own reading, drawing and homework in another corner.

Angelica and Hanna had found the concept of a Magazine much more interesting than Book Club, and Sue was fine with joining that, too. Sue had suggested starting a school newspaper but her friends liked the idea of a magazine, with lots of pictures and fashion and gossip sections. Sue and Harry would add book reviews, and Jacky could contribute comics. Sue had suggested naming their publication-to-be, Semblances, like the name of their school and town. The word means, appearances. But the group had settled on *The Freep*.

Hanna said, "Well honestly, I'm fine with not going back. I hope we're off until winter break. We will have even more time for our projects. We can meet at the library."

The girls all stared at her, remembering their afternoon. Then Sue had a brainstorm. "Hey! We could be investigative reporters, and write it up for the magazine! Why don't we do a story on the library?"

Chapter 9

Haunted

Joella jumped up and down and interrupted, "Did you tell your parents about what happened at the library?"

Hanna rolled her eyes. "Tell what. That we saw a movie, the power went out and back on again."

Angelica added, "Yeah, I did tell, but it just didn't sound weird to my parents." She was threading her fingers through her hair to brush sand or salt away from her scalp. She lived on the street nearest the beach and the stuff was always in the wind, in your hair, in your toes and in the carpet.

Hanna made another point. "And honestly, it's better not to tell even if it was actually weird, because they wouldn't let us go again, and then here we are with nothing to do and nowhere to go."

"But for the magazine—we could tell the truth. It would sound scary and increase circulation." Sue was on a roll.

"Ok, let's list stuff we know about the library. I mean, if you think about it, it's not like there isn't always weird stuff happening there," Angelica suggested. "It's so old, of course it must be haunted."

"We heard Georgie crying in the chimney, when he got hurt!" Joella jumped up and down. The other girls looked at her doubtfully, though they had heard something there too, in the end.

"The doors randomly lock and open."

"That skunk. Sometimes the smell follows you around the library and then disappears. And we've never seen it."

"Sometimes it smells like someone has been drinking, or smoking. Then it doesn't."

They all looked at Hanna after she said this, thinking about whether they themselves would know what the smell of drinking was.

"Books fly off the shelves sometimes." The children went silent with sudden recognition, and shivered.

"Have you ever driven by at night, after it is closed? Sometimes there are random lights on, upstairs. Once I saw light coming out of the chimney, like a fire in the fireplace!" This was getting to be like a ghost story you exaggerated for a campfire tale.

"Nothing is as strange as Ms. Wanda." Sue was sorry as soon as she said this because it sounded mean. Sometimes she tried to fit in by saying something quirky she thought her friends would like, but she often meant something different than the words sounded after they were spoken. She thought of Rowan's opinion about everyone being equally strange. Strangers are strange until you know them, then they're just your crazy family.

Sue did not mention the new chimney in the middle of the roof, or the white box which arrived after the storm. She wasn't too sure about what she had seen.

The phone rang and they jumped. Joella answered it and shrieked, "Georgie!" She listened happily for a while, said, "We're fine!" and handed the phone to Sue, who went across the room to talk where it was quiet. When she hung up, the girls all agreed to meet at the library the next morning for further investigation of The Haunted Library for their start-up magazine. Angelica offered to bring her big sister's old phone to use as a camera, and Hanna and Angelica took off at a run as the street lights started flickering on.

After they had gone, Sue looked across and saw that the park bench had been vacated. She locked up the doors and turned to talk to Joella, tucked in again on the couch.

"So we are on our own tonight. When they get done at the hospital, Mom and Dad are staying at Grandma's tonight. Apparently there are flooded roads between here and the hospital, and they didn't want to take a chance in the dark. Georgie is fine. They are still waiting in the emergency room. He just stepped on a cat or something and fell on his head. And he has to get rabies shots."

"Oh no! He sounded ok, though."

"Yeah so, we don't have school so—we can stay up a little while; but are you coming with me in the morning?"

"To the library? Yeah-yah."

Even though both girls were wildly imaginative, neither of them were fraidy-cats, really, not even Joella; she just maneuvered for what she needed sometimes—food, sleep—by overacting. Nothing really bad had ever happened to them, and they weren't really expecting it to this time. Any potential for mishap, they characterized as adventure. Tomorrow would be an adventure, and they would keep a diary of it for *The Freep*.

Chapter 10
Reflection and Refraction

Sue called Harry in case he wanted to come to the library tomorrow and do magazine work. He would come as soon as he could.

When Joella dozed off, Sue tucked the afghan round her and took Dog with her out back to look at the stars. It was exciting to make her own decisions. This was her first overnight without adults. Their parents would leave them at home alone for shorter periods, (except they wouldn't make her responsible for Georgie, he was a handful, obviously). Sue was just the right age to babysit herself and not older like Angelica's sisters, whose parents had to watch even more closely. She was glad, though, to have Joella and Dog at home too.

The sky was so clear and the stars so sharp that night. The moon was nearly new, so the stars had less competition. It always felt so good to stretch and look way up and out, after a long day hunched over a desk or a book or a screen. She looked up at Cygnus the Swan. There he was, the Northern Cross, with the Summer Triangle. Cygnus the good friend, rescuing his friend Phaeton from the water. Phaeton had raced his chariot too near the sun which melted it, and Zeus punished him with a bolt which sent him to the bottom of the water. Poor Cygnus wanted to rescue Phaeton, so Zeus rewarded his friendship and turned Cygnus into a swan. A swan is a glorious symbol of sky, water and earth, at home in all. That's the mythology behind the constellation. Swans, the birds, are loyal to their own. They are deemed aggressive, but only in defending their family. Oh, and in fighting with other swans for scarce resources...

Sue also thought it thrilling that the bright star Deneb in the Cygnus constellation, would one day become the new North Star, in about 8,000 years. Because the earth is wobbly on its axis, our own Polaris moves away from North. Well actually, we are the ones moving.

It seemed the right time to bring out the telescope. The stars got better the later you could stay up, and it was already later than Sue usually could stay out.

Sue let Dog back in to snuggle with Joella and she went to her room to put some more clothes on. She loved dressing like an adventurer on an expedition. Any activity which requires any length of time staying outside, rather than just moving from here to there, requires you to dress warmly against the weather. Most kids wore basketball shorts over leggings with socks and slides, just to be dropped off and run from the car to the gym or the mall or wherever. She had learned from her grandmother to cover her head and ears, layer shirt and sweaters, and always have gloves with you. (The worst part of gloves was always leaving one behind everywhere you went, but, they didn't have to match at night, after all. You can't tell in the dark; you need light to see colors.) Back in the family room, one little lamp was on. Dog was already twitching in a dream. Sue quietly crept back outside, closing the door quietly with her gloved hand so as not to wake her sister.

Sue loved the dizzy feeling she got from trying to keep up with tracking the stars and planets as the heavens rotated through the night, east to west, just as if we really live inside a giant whirring clock. In mere minutes she would have to move the scope to keep tracking her planet.

It made her really feel like the ground was moving under her feet as the Earth rotated.

She didn't need her glasses out here because she could adjust the telescope lens for her eyesight; and anyway the light emitting and reflecting from objects she was viewing came from so very far away, her short sightedness was hardly significant. We are all short sighted when viewing the whole universe.

The trouble was, not only was it dark, her limited vision could make the things around her in the yard look really strange. Sometimes she wasn't even sure if something she stared at was moving or still. Sometimes when you look at something a long time it seems to move suddenly. In the bath, the black spot on a white tile looks like it's moving and must be a bug! No, that spot is always there. Could the appearance of movement just be because your focus was interrupted? Like a blip in the wi-fi connection. Or does your brain fill in the details it expects, as a service to you in case you missed something.

In any case it was very important, Sue knew, to put things away where you were used to them in daylight, because in the dark that was right for night viewing, you were bound to fall over something unexpectedly out of place.

Somewhere in the din of frogs and bugs whirring and chirping and clicking might have been a beeping, a wake up timer or car alarm.

Sue heard a scurrying under the shrubs. She turned her head without moving her feet. Dog started barking wildly from behind the storm door. A shadow blacker than the surrounding night rose up. With the light behind it from the kitchen window, the shadow seemed to have a pointy triangular shape at the top like a hood. The universe froze for a moment and Sue felt sick.

Chapter 11

Sneaking Out

The hood came closer and grabbed Sue's arm, with Joella's warm little hand; the little sister had wrapped herself in a blanket, one edge over her head like a giant scarf. "What's that star you're looking at tonight?" Sue gave her sister a quick hug, adjusted the scope for her and moved aside to let her see. "It's Saturn! I can see the rings. It's glowing!" It was the color of a giant yellow cat's eye rimmed by its rings. Then she looked at Sue. "There was a big wild bobcat on the windowsill looking in at me." Sue twisted her mouth skeptically and packed up the scope. They went into the house. Sue checked all the windows.

"You were sound asleep. It could have been a dream."

"It could have been..." Joella made the same squinty-eyed, twisty-mouth face Sue had.

The sisters left all the lights on downstairs and went up to the room they shared. So that Dog wouldn't have to choose between them, they all three curled up in Sue's bed and, surprisingly, fell right into dreamless sleep.

***

The next morning was a very strange color, as the sun struggled to light the world through a thick, dull, dirty looking mist. The outside of the windows and house was dripping wet. Sue had taken Shea out for the morning routine, and the dog had been hesitant about climbing down the porch steps. No wonder, truly you couldn't see a thing. The harder Sue strained to see flat out in front, the blanker the fog appeared. She waited on the porch for Dog. A reassuringly cheerful puff of steam exhausted from the house and curled out into the fog; Joella must have been in her morning shower, she and the pipes would be singing.

The phone started ringing. "Oh, hurry up, Dog!" She didn't want to miss the phone but where was Dog? She decided to trust Dog's good sense and ran in for the phone, as the door banged painfully on her heels.

Grandma was calling to check up on them, and inform them that their family was on the way home, after a pharmacy stop. They had rushed out early when Georgie woke up, and hadn't wanted to call quite so early.

Dog was on the porch, but strangely distracted by something behind him which Sue couldn't see. He growled a little then let out a warning bark, which was peculiarly muffled by the fog. She hung up and let him in and he rushed in to greet Joella in the kitchen, then raced around the house for three laps to dry off. Dog ate his breakfast while the girls ate their cereal, and then he went back to sleep, with one eye on them.

"I suppose we should really wait at home for the family. I wonder if they would want us to stay here," Sue spoke to her spoon. "I feel a little guilty about cutting out right now."

"But your friends are counting on us!" Joella lay one ear down on her folded arms and looked up at Sue.

The girls justified leaving. Their parents wanted them to keep their promises and to be responsible for completing their assignments. Sue just felt a bit guilty for not calling to ask permission. But if she had been told no—she really did not want to miss out on this adventure, or abandon her friends.

There was no need to worry her family while they were so preoccupied with Georgie and everything.

There was safety in numbers. There would have been no good reason to make them stay home—especially since their parents had not heard about new Ms. Wanda and how they had been locked in yesterday.

And there were good reasons to go. They might actually have a real news scoop that the kids at school would like to know! And Harry had agreed to come, for magazine work.

Plus who could know how long everyone would stay there; maybe they would still beat the family home.

The girls left a note on the table:

> We had to meet friends at the library to work
> on a project. Can't wait to see you later!

She signed it with a drawing of eyes behind eyeglasses and a smaller pair with long eyelashes.

When they got to the traffic light at Main and Culvert, in unspoken agreement without even having to discuss it, the girls turned to take their new, back way to the library, up past Rowan's house.

Chapter 12

Rowan vs. Ms. Wanda

As the fog lifted it grew quite warm, and they stopped to remove their rain jackets. Sue tied its arms around her shoulders and Joella dumped her backpack onto the sidewalk, stooping to stuff her rain jacket into it. As Joella was kneeling on the patchy conglomerate sidewalk, she was distracted first, by the sparkles of quartz in the sidewalk which caught the sun breaking out; then by a rustle of a cat which streaked ahead of them and into the shrubbery along the walk. "So many cats," she sighed, and scrambled up.

Rowan's street looked different climbing it from this side. There seemed fewer houses than they remembered, and no cars were parked on the street. It still looked like a ghost town; the windows in the houses were dark. There were odd pieces of furniture and toys on porches, but no people. The vacant lots between patches of houses were wild and dark and overgrown. The trees were twisted and choked with vines and the weeds waved over their heads up on the embankment. The air smelled brackish and especially oppressive since the morning's fog. The greenery smelled garbage-y instead of spicy sweet.

The animal which seemed to have followed them now scooted out of the bushes in a blur and leapt up the hill at Rowan's. Joella laughed. "Let's go up." They had been invited to stop by any time.

As they reached the top of the funny steps, they saw a long stick, a twigless, twisting tree branch, standing up in the middle of the yard clearing, sticking into the ground, the way branches did when they fell out of trees in a wind storm. Sue noticed there were no trees overhead here, and thought the stick odd. When she was little she had once seen a black snake standing up in the road like that. She stared to see if it moved.

Rowan was just coming out of the kitchen and stooped to put a bowl of something down outside for Acantha. She straightened up, put her hands on her hips and waited for them. Sue kept a fair distance from the standing stick as she climbed up to Rowan. When she looked back, the stick was gone. Rowan turned her nose toward the sky and shook out her hair, then looked at Sue.

"Rowan, would you like to join us at the library today?" Sue was afraid to tell her their plans about investigating ghosts for *The Freep*, it might sound babyish.

To Sue's surprise, Rowan said, "Sure. Let's go." Joella grinned and took Rowan's hand, leading her back down the walk. Sue looked back at Rowan's house; no one was to be seen, and Rowan hadn't checked the door, spoken to anyone or left a note. They all went single file down the crumbling, curving stone steps to the sidewalk.

With Rowan, the tree tunnel seemed fresher. Here the leaves on the tulip trees cheerily waved back and forth like mittened hands in greeting. Newly turning red and yellow autumn leaves studded the boxwood shrubs all over, like Christmas tree ornaments. They still did not see anyone. Sue thought a lot of old people must live here. Maybe the old toys lying about on porches were for grandchildren when they visited, because they certainly couldn't see or hear any children's voices. Most of the family neighborhoods around here were never quiet; there were always cars zooming and shrieks and screams coming from somewhere, even in the winter in the silent snow. A few silent neighborhoods held great houses and long driveways, where everyone was gone for long days at work and day care, but even at those times one could count on crews of workers mowing, blowing, washing. Except not here. Rowan and the cat or whatever Acantha was, were the only lives they'd seen or heard. But that was only since yesterday, after all.

Rowan was quiet, while Joella filled in all the space with a chattering lecture of facts about bobcats and other native animals, until they saw the back of the library and its garden fence. Joella said, "I heard that this garden is really a graveyard of the Original People who owned this land!"

"No." Rowan was sure. "The ones who lived here first did not think anyone 'owned' land. And they would never have voluntarily left their own dead buried here, so it wasn't that kind of cemetery.

"That story they tell in school about the Vanderboor family who paid a native mere pennies for it? The buyers felt plenty guilty about taking advantage, but told themselves, well, the Indians hadn't demanded a higher price! And then, they figured they ought to have it, because they would wring more value from the land than the First People had done sharing it for hunting deer, turkeys and geese. The colonists made up lots of inscrutable legal papers giving themselves deeds, papers proving the transfer of ownership of the land, which meant nothing to the Native People. When the People tried to continue using the land in common with their new neighbors, they were killed as trespassers. Then the Vanderboors got rich when they sold the land. It was sold and bought and transferred from one white owner to the next and they would just prove their chain of title with the papers they had.

"If this was a graveyard, it wasn't intended by the people buried here. Maybe there are fallen dead here. The memorial paving stones aren't as old as that, though." It was the longest speech Rowan had made in their company. The three stopped and looked between the iron bars at the patches of flowers and paved walks which bore etched letters of quotes and memorials, stones sold to families as a fundraiser to support the library. The law office employing Sue's dad had one there, like a gravestone business card.

Sue added brightly, "It's kind of nice that the library made it up to them. That it's public space again, with stuff we share."

The girls circled the gated garden and walked up the ramp to the rear door of the library. There were no slugs today. It was just opening time. Sue and Joella were almost afraid to try the door this time, so they hung back a beat as Rowan stepped forward. The door opened out silently and they followed Rowan inside.

There seemed to be a lot of noisy hammering in the adult reading room, and a carpenter was crouched in its entryway prying up a floorboard. "Stay away from the repairs!" Ms. Wanda warned. She stood at the front desk and she opened her eyes wider than wide, as if she was not only looking but imbibing as much sensory information of them as she could, through her eyeballs. Then she narrowed them quite suddenly behind her glasses. Rowan stood facing Ms. Wanda at the desk.

"Hi," Sue breathed in the direction of the front desk, and walked quickly to the children's room, followed by Joella and then Rowan. They found Angelica fidgeting at a table. When she saw them she waved them over excitedly. Her eyebrows shot up when she saw Rowan with them. Rowan ducked off into the young adult aisles to browse.

"Look at this picture I got! Isn't it perfect for our paranormal library issue/welcome Ms. Wanda?" Three heads peered at the cracked phone Angelica held up.

"Weird!" In the photograph, the library chandelier was a shadow right behind Ms. Wanda's grinning head, and the eight darkened brass branches of the light fixture looked exactly like a gigantic spider coming to eat them with Ms. Wanda's teeth. "That is perfect! That is odd that the picture came out like that."

"My sister says that sometimes ghosts and stuff show up in pictures that you can't see with the naked eye. That's how her phone got cracked—she was so surprised about some of the pics on here that she dropped it."

"Uh huh." Jacky had arrived! He grabbed the phone from Angelica, and a joyful play chase through the stacks ensued, until Ms. Wanda entered the room. The children froze and plopped at a table and Jacky kept going, veering right out the door while announcing he'd be back.

Ms. Wanda came to the table and put both skinny wrinkled hands flat upon it, leaning down and staring beadily at Sue. "That girl you brought to the library. You should not hang around with that type. She has no supervision at home. She is a bad influence! You should stay with kids your own age." Talking about one kid's private life in front of other kids was a severe breach of teacher code, and the girls fell back a little with the smack of it, but it wasn't unheard of, even for teachers.

Before they could sort through and comprehend this warning, Rowan stepped out suddenly from behind the graphic novels shelf. She looked expressionlessly beyond Ms. Wanda at the white box still upon the librarian's desk. Her hair shimmered around her head like a helmet. Ms. Wanda seemed to shrivel slightly in Rowan's presence. She retreated to the desk. Then she turned about on her soft silent cloth shoes and floated back up the steps toward the front desk, holding the white box carefully before her like a cake.

Chapter 13

Digging

When Ms. Wanda was gone, Angelica laughed to break the spell. Rowan turned and looked at her for a moment, and said, "I've found what I came for. I have to be getting back home." She blinked a few times and grinned at them. "Have no fear!" She stuffed something into her pocket as she turned away from them, then turned back. "Oh, you should check these out." She placed an assortment of books on their table.

Angelica stared after her and then looked quizzically at Sue. Joella opened the books and shut them without interest. She ran over to a favorite shelf and sat on the floor there, leaning into a book. Angelica got up and wandered out into the library. Sue tried reading one of the books. One of them was a thick comic book, but looked like a more mature theme than she typically permitted herself. She tucked it underneath for later. Another was a dusty old history of colonial times, and the last was a random holidays cookbook. She put them away for later to try to understand the connection. Maybe Rowan had been kidding her, and the books had nothing to do with her, had absolutely no message for Sue.

Sue forlornly watched Joella pulling down books and suddenly realized Harry was at the front desk. Ms. Wanda had vanished. He looked up at her and waved excitedly. He ran loping down to Sue's table.

"No one is up there, I'll check out later. Hey, I found materials for our local history project! You have to see these." Harry sat down and thumped a pile of very large, very old books. The covers were woven cloth and slightly glossy with grime and wear. Sue opened one up and the pages were stiff and crinkly. An occasional dog-eared page was broken off at the fold. The dusty smell made Sue cough.

"Where did you get these?"

"There's a nearly empty return cart in the back adult reading room, and these were on it. It was facing the wall but I was trying to find a fishing book on the bottom shelf and when I pulled the cart away, I saw these. I don't know where they were shelved." The books had no call numbers printed on them. Maybe they were reference, but they weren't marked.

"Maybe they were somebody's books from home—donations for the book sale, maybe? "

There was a book of *Recipes and Spells*, with strange diagrams through many of the pages. There was a book called *Roosters*, but the pictures were not of chickens, but old pictures of old men dressed up in old suits standing stiffly and cockily. One of the books though was *How We Got Rich On Post Road*, and had a picture of their library on the cover, with a strange woman staring out the window.

"They look kind of boring. Except maybe these spells."

"I thought this one was neat. Look at this woman at the window."

Sue peered at the picture. "Hey! That looks just like Ms. Wanda! It can't be her, this is like 300 years ago! I wonder if she is a relative or something?"

"Creepy, right? I'm going to read this one. I'll report back next meeting. Gee, where is the staff? I have only seen Ms. Wanda, and now even she isn't around. How about I just 'borrow' these without checking them out? They don't even have bar codes anywhere that I can see. I bet they're donations. I'll bring them back, they will never be missed. The book sale isn't for months."

"Harry, that is so unlike you! I bet that is what happens every time they're looking for a book supposedly on the shelf, and can't find it. Someone 'borrows' it without checking out."

Sue followed Harry up into the central check-out room. True, no one was around. The repairs in the reading room seemed to have been abandoned. Harry slipped out the front door with a grin and a wave. Sue waited and browsed the music and movie recordings and video game bins. No one came. Joella slipped past her into the reading room across the hall.

Sue followed and found Angelica and Hanna leafing through magazines in the adult reading room. Already their legs felt too long for the little chairs in the youth section, so they often moved to the reading room. They sat around one end of a long table in bony Windsor chairs. Joella was walking around the room running her fingers lightly over everything. When she saw Sue she dropped into a chair. Sue nearly tripped as she entered on the edge of a loose floorboard.

A tall, lighted glass case held fragments of pottery and arrowheads dug up on the library's site. Hanna was sitting with her back up to the case but stood up and moved suddenly to a side chair across the table from it. Eyeing the tall case she marveled, "You are all so careless here. You take for granted all the time that all your fragile stuff will be safe."

Sue swiveled to look at the cabinet. "What is that stuff, anyway?"

"I don't mean this, particularly. I mean, wherever you are, at home. Your shelves are just loaded with breakable things. You put your mug down on the very edge of a table. Gravity alone could walk it right over onto the floor. At home, we had earthquakes. Not only would your things have been broken, people would be buried under your shelves of stuff. You don't know how carelessly you get by."

Angelica picked up the phone camera and snapped the cabinet, then returned to her magazine. Sue hunched down into her shoulders and looked down at her book. Joella popped up and pressed her nose and fingers to the glass of the case, peering in.

That's when Jacky came barreling in. He always moved kind of like a crazed creature in old cartoons, like a whirlwind, some combination of leaping and running even when he walked, limbs everywhere. More like, when two people scuffle in a comic strip and all you see is a swirl of dust with arms and legs sticking out, except Jacky was both people. He usually slapped the top of the doorframe when he entered a room. He also managed to trip over things a lot and he did now, face forward, but rolling to a standing position. A book jumped off the shelf onto the floor.

"Wow! Come look out the back window! Get a picture, Anj." Angelica followed Jacky to the back community room. Sue picked up the book. It was that biography again. She dropped it onto her pile on the table with her backpack and hurried after them with Joella.

Outside in the library back garden, Ms. Wanda stood by as a laborer dug up a section of memorial paving stones, in what the children just knew was a graveyard.

Chapter 14

Borrow or Steal

"**W**hat do you think they are doing?" The worker in a dirty coverall had his back to them and was bent over the shovel. He may or may not have been the same man who had been hammering at the floor earlier. Angelica surreptitiously snuck a photo just as Ms. Wanda turned from her examination of the hole in the garden to stare at the window with an annoyed look. Angelica and Jacky ducked.

"Let's leave now and walk around back to see what's happening," Angelica suggested.

"She just saw us. We need to play it casual for a little while." They traipsed back to the reading room.

Joella was already there, examining the glass case again. Hanna picked up her things. "I'm gonna head out and around back to look." Sue quickly grabbed up her armful of books.

"Me too!" Angelica and Jacky's whirlwind swept out together.

Then the glass case tipped forwarded and crashed down.

"Oh, Jo, what did you do?"

"I didn't do anything!" Joella ran from the room, screaming and crying.

"What have you children done?" Ms. Wanda entered the room screaming. "We will have to make the reading room off limits to people under the age of 24. Get out!" The door was creakily, squeakily shut on them.

"I'm sorry, Ms. Wanda..." Sue spoke to the closed door.

Sue turned worriedly to find Joella, who had run up the staircase. Sue quietly crept up. Joella was sitting on the hearthstone in front of the fireplace.

"What are you doing? This is not like you, to come up here?"

"I am listening to see if I hear that child. I thought I saw a girl at the top of the stairs come in here, and I ran up to see if it was Hanna. But no one is here."

Sue sighed. "Hanna left earlier, remember? Let's get out of here before anything else happens. I just have to check out my books." They clumped downstairs.

From the foyer hallway at the foot of the stairs, they could see that there was no one at the checkout desk. The reading room door was still shut. Sue didn't really feel like bothering Ms. Wanda right now. She wanted to go home. But she had to check out Rowan's book recommendations.

She suddenly felt desperate and daring. She shoved the books into her backpack to borrow them, Harry style.

Sue and Joella tumbled out of the library's front door. "Let's take the shortest way home!" They carefully walked to the crosswalk.

Joella tugged at Sue's sleeve. "Sue, there's a man in a car parked across the street. He is just watching the library. No, don't turn and look!"

At the crosswalk they waited for a car to stop and walked quickly across, and without turning her head Sue ran her eyes only over the street. Sure enough, a man in a dark hat appeared to be staring at them. He didn't wave or smile. When they reached the sidewalk the girls, by unspoken agreement, broke into a run on the sidewalk all the way down Church Street towards home.

They ran right into Ms. Kaycee!

"Whoa," Ms. Kaycee said, laughing.

"Ms. Kaycee, you're back!" Joella threw her arms around the beloved librarian.

She looked at them, puzzled. "Well, I'm just out to pick up lunch for my family. I'll be at the library when it reopens next week."

The girls looked at each other. Then it all spilled out and they told her all about Ms. Wanda.

Ms. Kaycee shook her head. "I think you're telling me a very good story, but the library has been closed, just like your school. I don't know any Wanda."

Chapter 15

Clues

S ue and Joella wanted to drag her back to the library with them but Ms. Kaycee laughed and said she couldn't right now. "I'll see you next week. I bet we will be super busy with school closed!" The girls sweetly waved good-bye and took off to their own house.

"Maybe she just didn't know, since she was off?" Sue shook her head as they ran up their front steps. "Georgie!"

They ran into the little television parlor adjoining the kitchen, followed by Dog. Georgie was covered with little bandages stuck all over, but they knew those were mostly for healing his feelings. After a lot of hugging the whole family shared sandwiches and sympathy for Georgie's experience. The girls were too tired to even try to explain the weirdness at the library, and stuck to making a fuss over their little brother.

That evening, Joella and Georgie were playing a game, and Sue looked through her books while her parents read their mail and the newspapers. What? Not only did she have the books Rowan gave her, but the adult biography which kept jumping off the shelf was here too! She must not have noticed when she picked up the pile from the table and stuffed them into her bag without checking out.

Their father snapped the paper. "Hmm. You'll be interested in this. There's an article in here about the Semblance Library. Seems the Board may have to shut the library. There's an issue with county and state funding for it, since they have to register a certain number of daily users to justify staying open."

"Oh, that is such a shame. Right when school's closed?" Their mother shook her head. "How's your project going, Sue?"

"When is it closing?" shrieked Sue.

"There's no date yet. The Board will have a public meeting about it in November. So you have time! Better go to the library! They count people who enter the library, and also the circulation of books. So better check

out another pile!" Her father looked at her pile of books
and laughed. Sue blushed.

She took her books to her room and spread them out
around her. The biography was just an adult book, with
an old photo on the cover of a woman in slinky clothes.
Smoked: Eunice Earley's Life and Legacy. Sue set that one
aside for now. She looked through the most interesting
one, the old holiday recipes, *A Spell of Cooking – Ready
for the Holy Days.* Curiously, there were a lot of pictures
of jars with herbal remedies which looked like the jars
at Rowan's house, with lists of plants or, who knows,
animals, in Latin or some language. There were also
jars with just stones and sticks inside, with titles like
"Guardian" or "Disguise", or "Win your Desire". These
seemed like lists of minerals and directions for order and
placement. Most everything included a little poem or
other words to say.

Sue looked closer and her mouth fell open. There was
the rhyme from the library:

The Winding

Sticks, bricks, iron and bone.
  Mud, rock, sand and foam.
  Leaves rattle, snows fall.
  Hide behind the chimney wall.

Look within, look without,
Close your eyes and turn about.
Inch by inch, going home,
Turn and twist, gift or loan.

Mud, rock, sand and foam,
Sticks, bricks, iron and bone.
—Traditional

Now whatever did that mean?

Sue had a sudden thought. She looked around her room at things that were from sticks of wood—her chair? pencils? Brick—she stared at the walls, wondering if there were bricks somewhere within? or the chimney that was exposed downstairs, covered with wallboard here; she let her mind rise up through the ceiling to the chimney on the roof. Iron? She looked under the covers and touched the bed frame. Bone—do the seashells on her desk count? She tapped her own teeth with her fingernail. There was *mud* in the garden, right up against the *rock* covering her hamster's grave. Or maybe the concrete and conglomerate rock foundation. Concrete was sand? Plenty of sand and foam at the beach; maybe they should try this there. Anyway, to practice: she closed her eyes and turned ...

Just then Joella tumbled into the room. She saw Sue's books and said, "oh, yeah, I almost forgot! Look what I have! It was in the library display case. I stuck it in my pocket to look at later. It's what I was trying to see when the case fell. And Sue: I saw a lady in a yellow dress reflected in the glass, when the case fell—" Joella ran to her backpack and drew out what appeared to be a scroll of stiff crackly very thin wood or very old paper.

"Joella, I can't believe you! This is like, historical or something. We don't want it to crumble into pieces!"

"But what if it is a clue?"

Sue thought, *look within, look without,* and took the scroll. She held it ever so carefully up to her eye and looked through it at Joella. Then she held it away and tried to see what was on the scroll on the inside. The outside did appear covered in old fashioned ink pen writing. The script was so decorative it was hard to read.

*Inch by inch, going home, turn and twis*t ... Sue very gently started to unpeel the scroll.

Chapter 16

Trust

S ue thought of the turning and twisting as she gently
pressed her fingers against the first half inch of the
wrapped up tight document. There were inked flourishes
of signatures which she couldn't really make out.

It didn't crack though. She carefully pushed the roll
back with one hand while smoothing the curly bottom
with her other hand. No, it was not the Declaration of
Independence. It was titled Deed. Six square acres of
land was transferred in exchange for a shovel made of
iron. Cornelis Hendricksen was to receive the full estate
of the land except Sam Lightfoot Sprekenduch was to
have "usufruct rights".

Joella hopped from foot to foot behind her. "What does it say? Is it a treasure map?"

"I don't know. How are we going to get it back to the library?"

"Ms. Kaycee!"

"We should keep a picture of this. For our research. Maybe Harry can make something of it."

Joella ran to get her kid's Instant Cam and clicked a picture, which was spit out on a little piece of paper. Sue put it in her backpack between the pages of one of her books.

When Sue's parents came in to say goodnight, she asked them, "What does use—usufruct mean?"

Her father laughed. "Where did you get that one?"

"We've been doing research on the history of our town for that project."

Her mother said, "Well, it means, the right to use something owned by someone else. For example, a life estate. A Will or a Deed can pass a property to someone who will own it fully and have the right to pass it on to heirs or to buyers, but can create a life estate in a person who has the right to live on the property during his or her lifetime."

The phone rang. It was Harry for Sue. Sue scrambled out to take the call. "Good night, Harry!" her mother called out, and her parents waved and shut the door to their room behind them.

"Sue, the library history is super interesting. Get this: none of the owners, since we have written records, seem to have kept the house long. The Breukelens were the last family to add on to the house to live in it, and as soon as it was finished they moved out within months. They didn't say why, but up to then there were a lot of rumors about strange noises, smells and beings. People stopped staying there when it was an inn as a result of the reputation, which was when it was turned into a private residence. Breukelen got it for cheap as a result, but suddenly sold it without making a profit.

"Eunice Earley, who was as frugal with her tobacco inheritance money as she was wealthy, bought it from him. Now it's in one of her trusts or something. A 'trust' holds something safe for someone else."

Sue opened her eyes wide. "Eunice Earley! That's the book that always falls on the floor at the library! I have it right here!" .

"Well, what does it say?"

"Well I haven't read it! I totally have it by accident. Hey, I wonder why they never tell us about the rumors of disturbances when we get the library history tour?"

"I imagine they don't want to scare us away, too!"

Sue decided she would ask her parents if they could help explain about Harry's information. Harry would write up his report for their Freep investigation.

"Hey. What if we could stay overnight at the library on our own, and see if any strange things happen? You know, be real investigative reporters."

"I don't know man, how could we do that? And wouldn't you be kinda scared?"

"I don't know. Of books falling on the floor? We could ask Ms. Kaycee to help us." They resolved to discuss it with the group and see if plans could be made. Sue returned to her bedroom, wondering.

The Eunice Earley bio suddenly became more interesting, but it was a thick book. Sue opened it to browse the table of contents and index for connections to the library, trusts, or ghosts. What she found made her freeze and her stomach flip in excitement—or dread.

Chapter 17

Defaced Public Property

I n the margins of the book, someone had written
notes in pencil. It wasn't unusual to see notes in a
book, (maybe strange for a library book), but these notes
were spaced throughout the book and seemed directed to
the reader rather than for the writer's benefit.

Sue thought this because the notes on many of the
pages began, *HELP ME!*

I am trapped.

Sue flipped the pages.

I am behind the wall.

Sue felt nervous. She had the urge to look around at her own room, but of course that couldn't be what was meant. She flipped more pages.

They took our home when we tried to share.

I am buried alive.

Please find me.

Sue couldn't read all the writing clearly. That could have been "buried" or "burned". At school, Sue's class was the final class year to learn cursive writing, and so she didn't have much opportunity to practice reading it. The writer wrote in a very cramped and hurried hand. Was she burned alive? Had she been a witch? Sue knew their local colonial tradition of witches was not to burn them, but there were lots of European immigrants since then, who might have brought their witch-burning traditions with them. Or was she buried, with the People in the garden? Sue didn't know how she knew the writer was a woman. She was probably influenced by the photos of

Eunice with her funny old fashioned face and swanky clothes. Or because she was thinking of witches.

Then Sue thought, this could definitely be a prank. It would actually make a good prank, to write messages in a library book to scare people who checked out the book. Hey, even to start a rumor of ghosts, at Halloween time...

It would also make a good way for a timid person to express a need for help. A sad person, if they weren't really sure they deserved help, might have left it for fate to bring the note to the right person, or not.

She definitely needed to bring this to Ms. Kaycee.

Sue flipped again to the photographs section at the center of the book. Eunice as a precious little girl with hair bow and pinafore. Eunice as a glamour girl getting out of a limousine. And there in a picture of Eunice Earley at a gala event supporting literacy and public libraries, was a small woman in a lady's suit, with her face scribbled out with a black pencil. Sue tried erasing the scribbling to see the person, but her pencil eraser just rubbed the paper right off. Now it was a weirdly faceless woman.

She had better make plans to return this to the library somehow without incriminating herself. Imagine if they thought she stole it, and wrote in it? She slammed the book shut and put it in her backpack, feeling terrible. She would definitely have to confess the erasure, at least. And, she supposed then, the "borrowing" as well.

Now what about these other, not-checked-out books which Rowan had chosen?

The spine was broken on the *Pictorial History of an American Township*, and some of the pages were loose or missing. Sure enough, it was about their town, Semblance, which was originally called Wobanak. The beginning of the book was just maps, and drawings of settlers in colonial dress doing business with the Original People, until over a hundred years later in the age of the first photographs. The town and city street pictures started in the 1850s.

There was the picture, like the cover of Harry's book about getting rich on the post road, of Ms. Wanda at the window of the library in the 19th century, when it was a residence and not a library. The caption said "unidentified woman".

She came to a picture of Eunice Earley as an old woman cutting a ribbon across the library portico, with the sign Semblance Free Public Library.

When she reopened the recipe book, a folded paper fell out. It was labeled Minutes, of an old library Board meeting from a few years ago. She opened it and skimmed over the formal rules of order language, until her eyes stopped on the list of persons present. Acantha Yazzie.

Wait, wasn't that Rowan's cat's name? Kaycee Bianco.
That was Ms. Kaycee. Wanda Withers? Hmm. The list
ended with Salvatore D'Amico, Earley Trust Agent.
The minutes included summary of a Trust report:

> ...by the terms of the trust, the use of the
> Semblance buildings as Library is granted
> only so long as the building continues in use
> as a free public library. Should the library
> be closed to the public for longer than two
> months, the property remainder will revert
> to the trust estate and any minor heirs of the
> life tenant. Upon the age of majority of the
> life tenant's heirs, or if no minor heirs of the
> life tenant be located, the property remainder
> shall vest in full fee to the trust and be sold,
> with fee of 6% to the Trustee, Agent and
> Manager of the Trust Estate, plus expenses
> and commission.

Gobbledygook. She read on to an interesting paragraph
in the Finance Committee Report:

> The troubling downward trend in visits by
> the public and circulation of books is of
> great concern. As the Board is aware, our

government funding grants are dependent on reporting numbers of users. The library is not sustainable without this funding.

Discussion: Members in attendance discussed how to increase circulation. Note was made of reports from adult and child library users that the library is "haunted", especially in evening hours. This may be the cause of decreasing attendance.

Sue jumped as Dog barked and growled at the window, at some shadow. She folded the paper and inserted it into the book.

She would research this further tomorrow. If she could fall asleep.

Chapter 18

Erased

The kids all resolved to meet at the library when it supposedly opened on Monday. Sue and Joella were dropped off by their mom, so they didn't have a chance to stop by Rowan's. As they approached the front door, Joella looked at Sue and pointed. The man in his car was parked out front again.

"Mom! Go around the block to the side please, so we can go in the back door?" Sue yelled.

Mom looked at her in the rearview with surprise. "Okay. That's an easier left turn for me when I leave, anyway."

From the side street they noticed many of the back garden pavers had been dug up and loosely dumped back in place. There were orange cones and yellow tape around this part of the garden. The girls got into the back door without incident, and waved off their mom.

Ms. Kaycee greeted them from the front desk, and they resumed their questions. Ms. Kaycee responded patiently.

"I don't understand. As I told you the library really was closed last week. I don't know any Wanda. I don't know why the garden is dug up, but perhaps they used the closing time to do repairs. As for the glass artifacts case, yes, the storm must have caused a quaking or gust of wind, and we found the case shattered. We've put away the historical artifacts for now."

Joella's eyes got big and she pressed her lips together. She looked like she was about to explode. Sue said, "Um, we found this. On the floor." She didn't say when. She handed the little scroll to Ms. Kaycee who took it, looked at it in puzzlement, and slipped it into the desk drawer for now.

"Can I take your books for return?"

"Uh, no, we are going to work on a project today with our friends. Thank you." Ms. Kaycee looked up their card on the computer and saw Joella's list of books about snakes and creatures, and that they weren't overdue. She laughed.

"Come on," said Hanna from the doorway. Sue and Joella rushed into the youth room. Sue dropped her not-properly-checked-out borrowed books on the return cart while Ms. Kaycee was bending over one of the public computers.

The whole press was there, Angelica and Jacky and Harry. Harry excitedly showed them what he had written about the history of ownership of the library and that their own library was really part of the famous Eunice Earley's trust estate, neighbor to the great gardens and museums she had left in trust for the public after her death. Joella fiddled with the choices in a pencil pot on the table, and Jacky and Angelica were doodling on each other's notebooks. Hanna seemed a little off. She seemed suddenly older and slightly removed from them.

"Ok, I have these. The book that jumps off the shelf, and the books Rowan wanted me to have. There was a paper in one of them! Oh, wait—" Sue ran back to the book return cart, grabbed her books and returned. She opened the Earley biography. "Someone wrote a note asking for help in the margins!" She opened the book. "I don't get it. I can't find the pages." She looked at a few pages where the book fell open from her use last night. "I think it's been erased?"

"Maybe you dreamed it?" Sue frowned at Harry's question. She shook out the other books. The loose paper of library minutes and the picture of the scroll were gone, too.

"Well the paper's not here either. Maybe Ms. Kaycee took it? That was pretty fast though. So we can't copy it exactly for *The Freep*, but I can tell you what I remember about it. People think the library is haunted, so some people won't come."

"I bet more kids will come if they hear it's haunted!" Jacky laughed, and Angelica nodded agreement.

Chapter 19
Set Up

"And if not enough people visit the library, it won't get funding anymore and the library will close, and be returned to—someone else. Or sold. Those were minutes from a meeting a few years ago already. My dad said this stuff is in the news again, what to do about the library, and there's a public board meeting coming up this fall."

"Let's have a sleepover here and investigate," Joella whispered. Harry and Sue looked at each other. She had read their minds, or overheard their telephone conversation.

Hanna agreed, "Yes. I would stay all week!"

Angelica said, "Yeah, maybe..."

Jacky banged the table with both hands. "Yes!"

They appointed Harry their spokesperson to ask Ms. Kaycee, and they all trooped with him to the front desk. Sue asked first, "Ms. Kaycee, where is everyone? I mean, is there anyone else working here today? There never seems to be anyone to help you anymore."

Ms. Kaycee sighed and said, "Yes, that is why we had to close during my vacation. We had to cut back on expenses. And it's hard to hire people right now without paying a market wage. So it's just me for now. I'm here only because I love the library! Don't worry, I have a panic button to use in emergencies!" She laughed, raised her eyebrows at them and patted her desk drawer.

"Ms. Kaycee, have you seen any ghosts in the library?" Joella inserted herself in front of Harry and Sue and peered up over the desk.

"Ghosts! Certainly not!" Ms. Kaycee laughed. "I don't believe in ghosts. You know, I'm a mother now. I don't get scared anymore, I don't have that luxury! I know it's fun to pretend. I do smell funny things in here sometimes, like cigarette smoke, when there is no smoking in the library. I've never caught anyone. I've actually been embarrassed that someone would think I've been smoking when it happens, all of a sudden, in the children's room no less! I don't smoke, though!"

Harry launched into his speech. "Ms. Kaycee. We need to stay overnight in the library. We are doing an investigatory research article for our school club magazine, *The Freep*. Short for The Free Press? We heard rumors about this building being haunted and we wanted a chance to experience this. If nothing happens, we would document the evening for our readers. We would be very respectful of course during our use of the library."

Ms. Kaycee laughed. "I'm afraid I can't offer you an overnight at the library right now. I'll tell you what: I can stay late with you after closing one night, say, until 11 p.m.? That would be like a sleepover, right? And I would need permission slips from all your parents."

"How about until after midnight? That's when spooky things happen. Like, 12:30?" Hanna insisted.

Ms. Kaycee laughed some more. "I doubt any of you will make it that late! I'm not sure I can! And your parents don't want to be picking you up at that hour! In fact, maybe 10:30 would be better..."

"Eleven it is! Thanks, Ms. Kaycee! When?"

Ms. Kaycee said she would have to check with her husband, but Friday should work. The library closed early on Friday, so they would have lots of time. And she would need another adult chaperone. Angelica offered her older sister.

They trooped into the reading room and took chairs around the long table. Hanna grabbed the young adult graphic novel from Sue's pile and buried herself in it.

"Rowan recommended that. Let me know if there's anything interesting in it," Sue told Hanna.

"It's about a witch," Hanna responded, turning the page and reading.

Harry rewrote his article so far about the library history, to include Sue's latest information. They were unsure what to do about the notes in the margins which disappeared. Hey, that's a good story though, they would report it just like that. They would attribute the story to "one witness", to show it wasn't verified, and so as not to embarrass Sue.

Sue wrote up a little something about the original inhabitants of the area, the sale of the land for an iron shovel, and asking the questions about the story Rowan had told about a possible cemetery in the garden.

Angelica was taking pictures with her sister's phone, of where the library case had been which was gone, of the loose floorboards, and was headed back to the community room with Jacky, to get pictures of the work on the garden.

No one else was seen to enter the library that day. Of course parents were working. After five would ordinarily be the busy time.

Harry said he was headed home. Hanna said she was staying as long as possible, alone if necessary. Sue wondered where Joella had gone. Ms. Kaycee entered with permission slips she had typed up permitting the child to stay at the library after hours on (date). At the bottom after the signature line was a strip in capital letters, PICK UP TIME IS 11:00 P.M.

They heard Angelica scream.

Chapter 20

Ghost

E ven though they assumed Jacky was doing something to frighten them, Sue and Ms. Kaycee ran to the community room. The lights were off. Angelica and Jacky were staring at each other in shock. They turned to Ms. Kaycee.

"A woman walked through here, and then just disappeared at the wall!"

"She was wearing, like, an old fashioned yellow dress. Her hair was all sparkly-like."

"Ok, enough with the ghosts. I don't know if this is such a good idea," frowned Ms. Kaycee.

"They're making it up to scare us," Sue suggested.

"You got me," Jacky said. Angelica looked at him in surprise.

They all returned to the reading room and each took one of the permission slips. Ms. Kaycee shook her head, said, "Don't make me sorry," and returned to her desk.

Jacky whispered, "No, it really happened, but I was afraid Ms. Kaycee would call off our thing."

"What happened?" Hanna asked. Jacky and Angelica told her the story in whispers. Hanna shrugged. "Did you get a picture?"

Angelica and Jacky looked at each other in dismay. "I was too surprised! I didn't even think of it!" They resolved to head home to eat. Hanna said she was staying. She was halfway through the witch's story.

Sue went looking for Joella, and sighed. The library sure did have a lot of disappearing people today. Wasn't it always kind of like that, with all the bookcases and corners. Weren't their nerves just on edge? She turned at last to the staircase under the spidery chandelier in the front hall, and climbed up. "Again? What are you doing?"

Joella was sitting on the hearthstone in front of the fireplace. "I am listening for the child."

"Well did you hear anything?"

"Someone screamed."

"That was Angie and Jacky."

"I heard someone walking up stairs."

"That was me, silly. Come on, let's go get lunch." They clumped downstairs.

Hanna didn't look up from her book, just waved them off. They gathered up their stuff and some blank permission slips. They waved to Ms. Kaycee and exited the front door.

"We should visit Rowan."

"We should. Look, that man in the car is there, watching the library. Should we tell Ms. Kaycee?"

They went back in to report the situation. Ms. Kaycee called the police. They decided to wait and see what would happen.

It was such a small town, size wise, and so little going on ever that the police were always there in a moment. The police lived in town and everyone knew them. They tended only to bother people with traffic tickets who were just passing through from other places, not neighbors.

Two officers in bullet proof vests entered. It felt like they took up a lot more room than other people who would come to the library. They weren't big men, but they seemed to stand taller than other people. They spoke to Ms. Kaycee.

"We checked it out. He is doing his job. He has i.d. from the State Library. He has a clipboard and a click counter. He is just counting people who enter and exit. He says it's an audit to confirm your reporting of numbers is on the up and up." The officer lifted an eyebrow at Ms. Kaycee. "Feel free to confirm that with a phone call to his boss, and let us know if you have any more problems." Ms. Kaycee thanked them heartily; the officers took a walk through the library to check everywhere, and left.

"Well, you heard the man. I'll just confirm it, but it sounds right, now that he reminds me. Why don't you go out the back door anyway in the meantime."

"Ms. Kaycee! What's in that big white box?" Joella just came out with it. The box was sitting behind her on a shelf under the mantel of yet another sealed fireplace, the one at front desk checkout.

"Oh, it's just a historical costume, for a reenactor we had here. I have to put it away into storage. Have a good day, now."

They all waved and left through the back door, wandering around the perimeter of the back garden to get to Rowan's street.

"So, clearly Ms. Kaycee has no idea why a Ms. Wanda was here when the library was supposedly closed. She also apparently doesn't believe that we got in and that the whole thing happened. I wonder what that Wanda was looking for, digging up the stones in the back? Or what she was doing with that white box?

"Maybe we should plan on attending the next Library Board Meeting to find out. That would be good to report in *The Freep*, too."

Sue concluded her thinking aloud to her sister and lapsed into her usual meditative silence. Joella skipped ahead, peering through the fence at the paving stones and shovel resting by a tree. When Sue caught up, Joella skipped ahead again, until they were just about at Rowan's. Acantha or some shadowy animal in the undergrowth rustled past them up the hill. They both climbed the stony steps up to Rowan's yard.

Rowan was on her knees in the dirt in her garden, with a little trowel. Her eyes were closed. Sue and Joella stood in front of her and waited. She finished whispering something and opened her eyes slowly. She saw the girls and slowly stood up.

"I was giving thanks to the soil and asking for permission to take these," Rowan said in explanation, opening her dirty hand to show three pretty rocks. "Here, one for each of us; tell your stone a secret wish and put it in your pocket."

Joella asked, "Are you a witch?"

Chapter 21

Witch

"Witch?" Rowan scrunched up her face. "What do you think?"

"Well, you have a cat, or something. Acantha." Joella was implicitly asking a question—*what is Acantha?* But Rowan just laughed.

"And you have lots of jars of, maybe of spells and things. And this place feels—interesting. And—there's an eye on your hand!" Joella pointed to her own palm. Rowan held up her palm, where she wore an inked eye, henna or ballpoint they couldn't discern.

"And you gave me a book of spells, and a book about a witch." Sue decided to jump in, too.

Rowan looked at Sue. "Oh, so now I'm a witch. What, have you been listening to that Wanda bad mouth me, that I have no parents or family?

"Let me tell you something. Do you know what my name means? A rowan is a holy tree. For centuries people planted a rowan right by the front door of their home, to protect the house from witches and malevolent spirits. I am not a wicked witch, I want to be a healer. Someone who wards off ill will.

"And that is what my 'evil eye' is for, here. It's for—the next time we go to the library? Ms. Wanda strikes me as a danger."

Sue told Rowan that according to Ms. Kaycee, Ms. Wanda wasn't even real. That no such thing could have happened.

Rowan shook her head. "I don't know about Ms. Kaycee either, then."

Joella defended her Ms. Kaycee. "She doesn't want to believe. Because she's a mother. She can't show fear." Sue and Rowan looked at Joella. "I want tea now."

Rowan smiled and invited them to sit in the garden. She bopped into the house and returned with a tray of teacups, pot, honeypot, and sandwiches layered with green leaves and an orange-brown spread on thick homemade slices of bread. The girls were starved by now, and this was delicious. Joella usually eyed unfamiliar food with suspicion and picked apart sandwiches to eat each layer separately, but she didn't even hesitate. Sue stared at her sister while she munched her own sandwich hungrily. When they were through chewing, the tea was cool enough to gulp down all at once.

Sue retrieved a permission slip from her backpack. "Here, Rowan, we are spending the night on Friday at the library. It's a special program. We are looking for ghosts!"

Rowan looked at the form uncertainly. "I don't think I can get permission for this." Sue felt flabbergasted. Rowan seemed to do everything she wanted without any apparent deference to parents.

The girls gathered up their things and waved good-bye after thanks for the meal and their stone wishes.

On the way home, Joella held up her little stone and told Sue solemnly to bring hers, too, on Friday.

"Sue, are you scared?"

Sue looked at Joella and thought for a minute. "No, I don't think so. Ms. Kaycee isn't scared, and she works there, she would know if we had to be scared. Are you? You know, you don't have to come."

"You don't want me to come? You don't think I count, do you. You just want your friends there. They don't want me, do they?"

"No, no, of course we want you to come, Joella. We will list you as a contributor to the paper. You are the one who heard the child upstairs and saw the girl in the yellow dress, after all."

"Yeah, I better come, we need all the eyes we can get. I hope I don't fall asleep..."

Joella never said whether she was scared.

Chapter 22

Plot

F riday evening arrived. Sue was so excited for their after hours investigation at the library, she didn't know how she would sustain her energy all day just with waiting. Anticipation was high for everyone else in the group, too, as the phone was ringing all morning, with everyone sharing reminders for bringing permission slips, camera, notebook, flashlight, magnifying glass, binoculars, a blanket, refreshments. They'd resolved to wear sweats for ultimate comfort and protection. They'd ruled out bringing weapons.

Of course, Georgie also wanted to come. "Me too! Me too! I want to go too!" Dog barked and jumped happily, hoping to go too.

Their mother explained, "Georgie, this is the girls' special event, as part of their school project. You know you are not old enough. You know that when you are in school you will have your own projects. But until then, you have your own special things that your sisters are too old to do now, like your Kids Klub. Aren't you lucky?"

Georgie did like Kids Klub, where he had water and sand play and little kid sports clinics, with plenty of ball play, and paints and crafts times. The girls did wish they could join in these activities, and sometimes they all played Kids Klub together at home on weekends.

Anyway, his show was on soon and they were going to make popcorn. He hugged Shea and cuddled up on the couch with his gaming blanket and his monster pillow. Honestly, it was about his bedtime already.

It had been decided that the girls could go home with Angelica and her sister, since her sister was attending and driving, which made it so much easier. So they also packed any overnight things they would need. They could always drop Joella home if she panicked about sleeping over; in fact, Sue might encourage that option.

Hanna was already there. Ms. Kaycee was opening the door, her baby in her arms. "Oh, wouldn't you know, at the last I couldn't get someone to say with Lila. But that's all right, you don't mind if she comes too? We won't bother you, you do your research." Ms. Kaycee popped open a travel playpen next to her desk in the children's room. "Let's have your permission slips."

Jacky entered with Angelica and Doreen, her big sister. All the kids crowded around Ms. Kaycee's desk. Jacky waved a toy clown rattle at Lila in the playpen, who laughed and kicked her feet.

"Where's the bottom of the form?" Ms. Kaycee asked Jacky and Hanna.

"Oh, my parents cut the bottom off, the part with the time on it, to hang on the bulletin board." Hanna nodded her agreement. Just then Lila started wailing, and Ms. Kaycee shook her head, rolled her eyes and waved them off.

They spread their stuff out on the tables and floor. Ms. Kaycee said, "That's fine, you can camp out here, just keep all your food and drinks in this room, please." She had a quiet conversation with Doreen, who nodded several times. They both smiled, then Ms. Kaycee went up the stairs with Lila to walk her around the library a bit.

Hanna watched their exchange then said, "Doreen, you're so lucky to be grown up."

"Hmmph. Why? Not so lucky to be stuck here with you kids as if I'm somebody's parent, instead of out on a Friday night." She stuck out her tongue but then laughed with pleasure. "What snacks have you got?"

Joella unpacked a box of toaster pastries with enough packages for all.

"Ooh, I love those!" Everyone agreed. They tasted like raw pie dough filled with cinnamon-warm spread, even without heating them.

Joella crossed her arms. "Cinnamon makes people feel better," she stated with a firm nod. Sue gave her a sidelong look. She hoped tonight wasn't going to be a disaster.

They decided they would stay together, and start with the reading room, then the community room, known as The Club Room. Jacky readied his flashlight. Angie had her camera—well, Doreen's old phone. Harry had a notebook and his astronaut pen which could write even upside down. Sue had Joella's hand, and Hanna led the way, past the front checkout room. No one was there because the library was technically closed. Sue noticed the return carts had been emptied of books, which must have been re-shelved.

As they headed to the reading room, Angelica stopped at the foot of the staircase and photographed the spidery chandelier and the steps leading up to the darkened hallway at the top. They all then walked quietly into the reading room and stood for a moment unsure what they should actually do, now that they were here in the library at night. Ms. Kaycee popped her head in. "How we doing? I'm going to head up to the staff room to feed

Lila. I'll be back." Her steps creaked up the staircase until they couldn't hear anything more.

Doreen grabbed her choice of magazines and pulled out a chair. Angie snapped pics of where the glass case used to be, in front of the window. Then she folded up a corner of the throw rug now covering the bumpy entry way and photographed the uneven floor boards.

"All right, let's plan some things we need to get to tonight." They all huddled in a corner in the doorway just outside the reading room, out of Doreen's hearing.

Hanna said in a low voice, "I have to tell you something. I'm not going home tonight."

"What?" They all froze and looked at her. Sue felt a shiver working down her spine. Was that a prediction? or a plan?

"I'm going to pretend I'm leaving, then I am going to sneak back in and hide."

"What?!"

"I can't go home, guys. My uncle is there this weekend and...well, he's not very nice. I told them it was an overnight."

The group looked at her. Jacky fidgeted with the doorknob. No one knew quite what to say.

"We'll help you, Hanna. We'll stay with you."

"But—"

"Ok, here's what we'll do. I'll explain it to Doreen. She won't care. She was taking us all home anyway—"

"My parents are picking me up?" Harry said.

"Oh, sorry, Harry. We will all leave at the same time as you, Harry."

"Please don't say anything to Doreen until I 'leave'. I don't want to talk to her about it right now," Hanna pleaded.

Joella whispered to Sue, "But aren't we lying?"

Sue whispered back, uncomfortably, "Well, technically we told Mom and Dad we were staying with Angelica and Doreen. So, that is what we're doing..."

Doreen glanced over at them.

"Well, when shall we look for the ghost in the community room?" Harry said loudly.

Chapter 23

Ghost Trap

"**S**orry guys, I'm outta here." Hanna waved cheerfully at them and went looking for Ms. Kaycee to explain she had decided not to stay, and to walk home. Even though the library was officially closed, it wasn't so late yet, to walk home at this hour.

Just then, who should slip into the room with them but—

"Rowan!" Sue and Joella ran to greet her.

"I happened to get here when Hanna was opening the door to leave, so I was able to get in. I have my permission slip." Other than the slip of paper in her pocket, Rowan carried nothing.

"That's amazing!" Sue briefly filled her in on what they were doing. She didn't say anything about the books, right now. Rowan seemed especially...charged, tonight, or something. Her hair floated about her and seemed to move in nonexistent breezes. She wasn't even quite as tall as Sue, but she seemed the tallest. Her posture was very, very straight, as if she were suspended from her head and chin on marionette strings, her feet so light they barely brushed the floor. Sue didn't want to break the spell of Rowan's sudden appearance and her thrill that Rowan was joining in with their group.

"Okay, so, now?" Harry asked. Angelica and Jacky seemed a little worried about the community room, since their last experience had been the vision of that woman disappearing. Plus the lights weren't on back there. Ms. Kaycee hadn't put them on, and they didn't know how to. Though that was actually kind of convenient for their ghost investigation experience, made it that much more exciting a tale to retell. Harry, Joella and Jacky readied their flashlights, and Angelica had her phone camera. She took a photo directly at the flashlight beams reflected back at them off the glass French doors, from the dark hallway, then dropped back behind Jacky and the light.

"I know!" Sue had an idea. She held up her braceleted arm, bearing the black silk cord tied to each side of a silver washer, a flat wheel of metal. The Freep had had a fundraiser activity at school with these. A set of metal posts the size of large, thick nails, bore on each a molded letter of the alphabet, backwards, on the bottom. You took a hammer and banged on the post, and the letter was imprinted on your hoop of metal. This was how printing presses used to work; the typesetters arranged the letters into words which were inked and pressed into rolls of paper. They all had a bracelet with their word. Sue's was CURIOUS.

"We can tie a string from one bracelet to another bracelet across where you saw the ghostly woman walking, and loop each bracelet up around a chair leg. If there's a real ghost, she'll pass right through it, right? If it's a person...she'll trip?" Sue suggested. Rowan laughed. Sue blushed.

"Where would we get a string?" Angelica looked around at everyone.

"I have one! I picked it up from the secret stairs that time after the storm." Joella ran to her backpack and pulled out a piece of yarn coiled up. It was stiff like waxed twine, with dried glitter glue. It matched the yarn they had seen in the staff room upstairs next to the stairway which went nowhere. She gave it to Sue, with her bracelet, which bore the word THANKFUL.

Sue sat on the floor cross legged, tied the ends of the yarn to each bracelet and then scrambled up. "OK.

We can move the chairs the right distance to make this string taut. Show us where you saw the thing." She inserted herself behind the leaders holding their flashlights. When they approached the glass door to the dark community room, Harry shone his light into the room before opening the door. It reflected back at them off the glass with a spooky reflection of Sue's shining eyeglasses. The only other thing they could see was the lamppost light through the back window of the garden. It looked like another flashlight shining back at them. Harry opened the glass door to the dark community room and they all quietly filed in.

The room was creepy, being dark. A glass case held antique farm tools; the old photographs of sad children in smocks and stern adults looked mournful when the circles of light from the flashlights moved over them. Of course no one smiled for pictures in those days, because the exposure took so long; they had to hold still a very long time. Still there was usually someone a little blurry with fidgeting, and a few faces were blurs.

Jacky tipped up a chair for Sue to slide her bracelet up the leg, and put it down against the wall, then another, and together they slid one chair across the carpeting until the yarn was pulled tight, about two feet off the floor. Angelica took a photo. The flash made the rest of them jump. Rowan laughed.

"I hope our trap works. We'll wait, and find out if Angie and Jacky were just trying to scare us. Anyway, it makes for a good article for *The Freep*."

They were lined up at the window looking out at the garden and watching the bats materializing out of the darkness, swooping in to catch bugs near the lamppost and disappearing again. Jacky turned and grabbed Angelica's arm. They each swung around, except Joella whose attention was fixed on the bats.

There was a woman in an old fashioned yellow dress, with strange glittering hair. She floated slowly from one corner of the room, toward the front glass case, and right toward their trap.

Chapter 24

Overnight in the Library

Angelica's phone camera flashed. No one jumped this time; they were frozen to the floor. The woman kept floating forward. She passed the two chairs without disturbance and floated down behind the case on the front wall.

Just then, they heard a loud bang, coming from—everywhere. And a cry, and banging.

Sue grabbed Joella's hand and they all ran out of the room toward the light at the front of the library.

Another storm seemed to have descended over the library and the windows were rattling. As they neared the staircase, they heard banging upstairs. Sue felt much braver here, where the lights were on, or maybe there just wasn't time to think. They heard a muffled yelling from Ms. Kaycee and a baby crying upstairs as they ran up the staircase, two kids at a time, two steps at a time. Doreen pushed her way to the front of the pack and ran right down that long hallway to the Staff Only door, rattling the knob. It was locked.

"The door slammed shut and I can't seem to open it from inside!" It was Ms. Kaycee calling through the door, and banging on it.

"It seems to be locked," Doreen told her. "Do you know where there's a key?"

"I don't. We never lock this door. I will look around in here. Check the top front desk drawer in my desk downstairs, and at the check-out counter, and bring any and all keys you find."

"Ms. Kaycee, there was a ghost in the community room!"

"Maybe that's who slammed your door closed!"

"Right...well, let's get this door opened, first thing."

Doreen was already on her way downstairs. As the kids turned back down the hall toward the steps to look for a key, a bulb in the chandelier in the upstairs poetry room flickered, and drew Rowan's attention. She stopped at the door. She beckoned Sue to join her.

Sue stopped in horror behind Rowan. There was black grease writing on the mirror over the fireplace, where a candle burned in front of the mirror. The words were: GO AWAY. DON'T COME BACK HERE.

"Now who would light a candle in front of a mirror? Everyone knows that opens a portal for demons." Jacky elbowed through.

Angelica followed them in and took a picture. "Looks like someone is not too happy we're here."

Sue blew out the candle. "Ms. Kaycee will think we did that!"

"Let's get out of here." Angelica herded everyone into the hall and closed the door to the room. The room where Ms. Kaycee was trapped was quiet. They walked down the stairs to find Doreen. She had emptied the top drawer onto the desk and was pushing things around. Sue leaned in and noticed the scroll was no longer among the stuff. Angelica was thumbing through her phone pictures. "Whoa. Look at this!"

Their heads bowed down together over her phone. "No, wait, this one. This was the snap of the dark top of the stairs, from the bottom when we first started tonight. It's a woman!"

Joella said, "That's the girl I saw last time. I saw her in the glass case, too."

Rowan narrowed her eyes and looked closer. "Yellow dress."

"Like the ghost in the Club Room!" Angelica's eyes opened wide.

Joella said, "Oh, the Club Room! I saw someone out the window. In the garden. He had a pointy head and was all black." Everyone looked at her. No one really wanted to go back there right now to look for themselves.

"Here we are!" Ms. Kaycee and a sleeping Lila turned the corner from the center hallway and staircase. "I couldn't find a key, but I was able to open the door when I tried again, after all! Now what the—" She pulled a sticky, gluey piece of yarn off the bottom of her shoe and dropped it in the trashcan next to the desk. The kids looked at it but stayed quiet.

"Well, it seems to be almost eleven. How did you all make it so late without getting sleepy? I don't know about you, but I'm about ready to get out of here. I hope you had a good night, sorry I was absent for so long! Don't worry about all that stuff, Doreen, I'll get it tomorrow, just leave it exactly like that. Thank you for helping me. Now pack up your stuff, kids, and I'll wait for your parents with you."

No one brought up the mirror in the poetry room. They all silently decided to take Ms. Kaycee at her word, in the broadest sense: to leave everything until tomorrow.

Backpacks packed again, they all filed out the back door in front of Ms. Kaycee, who shut the locked door behind her. Doreen's car was there, and there was Harry's dad's car, engine running, headlights on.

Ms. Kaycee counted heads. "Hanna left earlier; as I recall, the rest of you are going home with Doreen, Doreen you're dropping Jacky, and Rowan? Harry? That your dad?"

Harry nodded and walked to the car. As his dad pulled away, he looked out the window at them mournfully and waved.

"Ok then, good luck with your reporting, kids. Hope it doesn't scare everyone away from the library! Good night!" She laughed and buckled Lila into her seat, who didn't even wake up with the jostling.

"Thank you so much, Ms. Kaycee! Good night!" The kids all called out their thanks while Doreen made a fuss about rearranging stuff in the back seat, and putting backpacks in the trunk. When they saw Ms. Kaycee pull off, Doreen straightened up and crossed her arms. The back door opened. Jacky shone a flashlight at the dark doorway. It was Hanna.

"Sh! Come on!" One by one they ran to the door, Rowan and then Jacky, Angelica, Sue clutching Joella's hand. Doreen was looking at the garden and the back of the library, and up to the roof. She slowly walked to the door, shaking her head.

"I don't know but...You know, it looks like there's a light coming out of the chimney, almost like there's a fire in there."

"Let's see! Hold the door!" The rest of them watched through a crack in the door as Angelica and Jacky ran out to the sidewalk, and Angelica snapped a picture, then they ran back.

Before Sue closed the door, she looked where Joella pointed. There was a dark figure with a pointy hat, and a small dark animal, scurrying away from the lamplight in the garden, toward the library.

Chapter 25

Turns

J ust then a downpour started, and Sue quickly shut
the door. The kids were in the dark. They didn't want
anyone to get suspicious about lights on in the library.
Sue told them about the figure in the garden.

"Don't worry about that. There's no law against
someone walking around town and cutting through
there, even at night." Rowan dismissed her concern,
and Sue felt embarrassed for joining in Joella's typical
nighttime monster tale.

They gathered around the front desk in the dark,
treasuring the dim light coming in at the skylight over
the door from the garden lamp. "I don't think you have a
ghost in the Club Room, either," Rowan added.

"But it walked through our trap and disappeared!"

"How?"

"Why?"

"I don't think so either," Joella pouted.

"What are you talking about?" Hanna looked confused. Angelica tried to show her a picture of the ghost they'd seen, but there was nothing there. The phone camera had flashed, and all they could see was the chair and wall as if it were daylight, and the corner of the glass case reflecting the flash. She tried to explain to Hanna what they had seen, and about Sue's ghost tripper trap. Hanna laughed.

"I'll show you." Rowan led the way and they felt their way through the hallway, with Jacky's flashlight shining down before their feet. They felt a little braver with skeptical Rowan in the lead.

"Look." She grabbed Jacky's hand and took the flashlight from him, shining it up at the ceiling. Track lights. But one of them was a round flat fixture. On one side was a small tube with a tiny lens on the end; in the depths of it shone a blinking red light.

"Huh?"

"It's a projector, like they have in school for the smart board. I'm betting your ghost lady was just a movie."

"But who made it go on?"

"I don't know. There may be a remote control. Or a timer. Or someone may have been in that closet." There were two doors in the room, one side was a closed door and the other side was the emergency exit.

"I don't want to open it in the dark," whispered Angelica, shaking her head.

"Everybody stand, like, behind the door on the hinge side. So you're behind the door when it opens. Somebody open and stay behind the door. I'll hide behind these chairs and shine the flashlight in." Jacky's plan wasn't too bad. When he had swished the light around and no one appeared inside the little room or large closet, Doreen peeked around the door and then waved the others in. There was a light switch which seemed okay to use because there were no windows in the closet. But they would have to close the door behind them!

Just library closet stuff. A little tea table, extra folding chairs, an old AV cart with a TV on it and a snarl of cords and wires on the middle shelf.

On the floor in the corner was another of those white boxes. Rowan stuck out her foot and lifted the lid off with the toe of her shoe, then bent down and drew out a very old, long yellow flowered dress.

"Looks like our ghost changes her wardrobe."

"Or it's a very old movie!" Joella jumped up and down nervously.

Jacky reached into the bottom of the box and pulled out a snarl of wool yarn with glitter dried into it. He laughed, put it on his head like a wig, and made a kissie face pose. Angelica snapped. They restored the costume to its box, shut the light and crept out into the dark community room again.

"That emergency exit reminds me. We should check those back rooms upstairs again, and the secret stairway. For any ghostly activity."

"You mean like, the writing on the mirror."

"What?" said Hanna.

"Are we ever going to be safe to sleep here?" Joella asked.

"Soon, Joella, I will sit with you."

"We can take turns watching!" Jacky offered.

"I don't think I could sleep!" Sue's mind was racing. "Ok, Joella, I have to think. The children's room is pretty quiet, when it comes to weird activity. I have to piece together what we know so far. You can sleep. Guys, what do you think about splitting up?"

"I'll stay with Joella," Doreen offered.

"Maybe we should stay together," Joella piped up nervously.

Sue chewed her thumbnail and looked at her. "Ok, how about we all go up to the poetry room?"

Hanna agreed. "We're safest up there, from anyone entering the main part of the library, especially if we are asleep in the morning. And from people looking in windows at us. Less noticeable up there."

Jacky wiggled excitedly. "Plus there's extra food, water, and an emergency exit, in the Staff Only room."

"You mean, we're taking refuge in the room that told us to Get Out..."Angelica objected.

"What?" Hanna shook her head and barreled on. "How about this: half of us will watch in Poetry, the rest of us will see what's down those stairs. Doreen and Joella and Sue, stay in Poetry; rest and think and collect what we know so far. We will take a turn exploring. Sounds like I missed a lot anyway, you can catch me up. Then we'll report back."

Joella demanded Rowan remain behind with them, or she wouldn't sleep a wink, and Rowan was agreeable, so they adjusted the groups accordingly. They went upstairs all together following a flashlight, ever so quietly, even though they were alone in the building. They spoke almost in whispers in the darkness.

"Hanna—where did you hide after you pretended to leave?"

"Oh! That was great. Ms. Kaycee was busy with the baby, I said I was going, I left out the front door and ran around the back. I watched from the window for when she was out of the front area. Then I came in the back door. I figured if I saw her I would say I forgot something. I didn't see anyone and went right up the stairs. I heard the baby in that other room so I took a chance on the

Staff Only door in the poetry reading room, and then I hung out on the secret stairs."

"Poor Hanna!"

"I had a book."

Chapter 26
Hearing Voices

"So the real question is: why? Why is someone showing us ghosts?" Sue chewed on her pencil at the table in the Poetry room, by the light of a little battery candle from the mantlepiece. None of them had matches to use the stump of real candle. Doreen and Rowan sat cross-legged on the floor where they settled with Joella on top of a pile of their sweatshirts and the pillows from the window seat. Rowan stared hard at the words on the mirror. They were on the floor at the long end of the table, in front of the window and away from the hard bricked up fireplace. Angelica, Jacky and Hanna were whooping it up in the Staff Only Room. At this point they had abandoned their reticent best behavior. They'd already rallied behind Hanna's overnight escape from home and technically, they were already breaking the rules. If ghosts were going to write in books and throw them around, lock doors and dig up the garden graveyard, well they could enjoy investigating the situation.

"It could just be random," Doreen suggested. "Maybe it's just an old library program stuck on play in the community room. It doesn't have to be intended for us."

Joella mumbled. "Who keeps locking the doors? Who locked the door on Ms. Kaycee before?"

Sue put down her pencil. "Maybe that was Ms. Kaycee? On purpose?"

Rowan narrowed her eyes and looked up at Sue. "Who is Ms. Wanda?" Just then a terrible smell hit them all and they all made the same face.

"Skunk!"

"Hey!" Jacky stuck his head in. "Just so you know. There is a window back here, mostly hidden behind the snacks cabinet. And—that thing with the pointy head is climbing up the fire escape in the back!"

Suddenly they heard voices. Talking. Right in the room with them. Two women were talking, plain, clear.

What did you bring me tonight?

*I thought you were hungry. There is something
special here.*

Why is there so much activity tonight?

The time grows short.

Rowan's eyes were wide with astonishment, and the
rest of them scrunched down their eyebrows and listened
hard. A smell of smoke wafted through the room, as if a
ghostly fire were lit on the hearth instead of a blank wall.

"Maybe we should get out of here." Doreen eyed the
fireplace nervously. "We could just all leave right now. You
can all stay over with us, or I can drop anyone home who
wants."

"Now? But we are getting some good stuff for *The
Freep*. We can't leave now. Just when it's getting good."
Everyone else agreed with Sue.

"The fireplace is sealed, right?" Jacky knocked on the
solid brick chimney. Not so solid. One of the bricks was
crumbling around the edges. He picked at it. He wiggled
it and was able to pry it out, like wiggling a loose tooth

until you get your fingers around it and pull it like a weed.

"Jacky! Put that back!" Doreen rolled her eyes and shook her head. Then Jacky spun around, holding up a key.

The Freep staff and friends silently came to one agreement. Jacky pocketed the key and opened the Staff Only Door, and they all joined Hanna and Angelica, who were crouching under the window. Angelica popped her head up.

"No, don't look!" Hanna snapped. "It's already up past us. I don't know what it is. I don't know why. I don't think there are any ways in up there."

"Through the chimney," Joella breathed.

"What did it look like?"

"Like, a black shadow, with a pointy top. It went up the building and disappeared at the top! And a little black cat or something ran along the roof top!" Angelica nodded agreement, and shivered.

Jacky turned to Angelica and Hanna. "And did you hear that, in the Poetry room? Disembodied voices!"

"I wrote it down." Sue held out her notebook for Hanna.

Hanna read it and said thoughtfully, "Let's move away from these voices. And the creature went up. Let's go down.

"You know, when I was hanging out on these stairs earlier, I was thinking...the one door we didn't try was the other door, all the way down. We could open it, peek, and then scoot back up and out the emergency door, if we need to."

"The cellar door?" Jacky and Angelica looked at each other. "The one that says Keep This Door Closed At All Times?"

"Well, how do we know where it leads? Is it the cellar?"

"It's below ground level."

Doreen said, "Look. I'll take Joella to the car, and have it ready right there on the side street by the garden, for our getaway. Take your picture or whatever, and then let's get out of here."

Joella brightened up with a second wind. "I'll ride shotgun! With Rowan!"

Doreen whispered behind her hand, "She'll be asleep in the back. Hurry up, but be careful! Angelica. I mean it. And don't leave anything behind! Or bring anything with you!" One big sister and one little sister went down the stairs. "I'm afraid to push the emergency door open, what if it alarms?"

"It didn't last time."

"What if it sounds at the fire station, instead of here? Or, it's on now, but wasn't during the day?"

"Then we all run, that's all."

Rowan spoke up. "I think we should go."

Doreen slowly touched the door handle. Then she turned back.

"Let's not risk it. We'll stay together." Joella giggled with relief.

Something went *bang!* behind them, upstairs. Rowan swiftly pushed through them and pushed the door wide, and she, Doreen and Joella exited.

The rest didn't follow. Instead they quietly and quickly started down the staircase to the emergency door landing. At the landing, the staircase down turned right to another landing, and right again until it was beneath them. They kept going, past the emergency exit; Rowan was out there holding the door for them, but carefully closed it from outside when Sue held a finger in front of her lips and pointed down the stairs.

They went down the stairs in pairs now. The Freep, minus Harry. Angelica and Jacky led the way down, Angie's phone light held high, and Jacky the flashlight, though they didn't need it here; the stairs glowed in the red emergency light over the exit sign. But they were prepared for the darkness below.

They stopped at the next landing, and looked down the next flight to the basement door. There was a shovel next to it.

Jacky reached in to open the cellar door, the one marked Keep This Door Closed... Angelica held the phone light high and swished it around the blackness.

This would have been really scary in the daytime, a completely dark basement when they didn't know where the light switch was; but they'd been in a dark library ever since Ms. Kaycee had gone, so it was kind of just another room at this point, no more or less scary than the rest of the dark and shadowy library.

A cricket or something jumped away from the moving circle of light and Jacky shrieked. "Good thing Joella's not here."

"Are you kidding, she'd love it."

"Well, good thing Doreen's not here," said Angelica, laughing with everyone. Her light stopped on the far wall. "What's that?"

Chapter 27

Secret Stairs

On the far side of the room was a smallish door, white painted wood, in a raw wood frame between it and the old brick wall. It had strange old black metal hinges and handle instead of a knob. Jacky and Angelica walked toward it, around the table of books, and the others followed to stay near their light. Angelica stopped to snap some pictures all around.

They heard voices again, muffled, coming toward them from the steps, where they'd left the door open for the light from the emergency exit.

"Oh no! What do we do?"

Hanna stepped forward and tried the door handle. It didn't budge the door. Jacky reached into his pocket and pulled out the old metal key. He held it up. "Make a lucky wish," he said, and jiggled the key into the lock above the door handle. Hanna jiggled and pulled the door, and it creaked open, scraping the dirt floor, until it stopped, jammed on the floor which seemed to have risen, unless the door sagged. "Quick!" Jacky waved them to follow, and squeezed himself through the opening. Hanna, Angelica, and Sue piled in, and Sue turned to pull the door closed.

"It's stuck." The door wouldn't budge to close. They looked wildly around where they were. Before them rose another staircase, but this one was a twisting metal stair. They looked up. It went up and up through a round cut in the ceiling. There wasn't really anywhere else to hide.

The four children climbed the cold, metal stairs as quickly as they could. Only one could fit at a time and Sue was in a panic as the one on the bottom, nearest whoever was following them. The stairs creaked and shuddered a little as their weight clomped down, turning, turning as they climbed to the circular opening above. What if something reached up and grabbed her by the foot, and pulled her down into that dark basement? Jacky's flashlight was tucked into his belt upside down behind her, shining down eerily on the children's faces. Angelica held her phone light up in one hand and onto the railing with the other. Sue just followed Hanna, keeping her eyes on the pompoms on the back of Hanna's socklette sticking out of each sneaker. She was afraid to look down.

When they reached the first hole, it was a room, but the stairs didn't end there. The staircase kept turning up and up. Jacky sat on the top edge now of the circle, which was a floor of a room. He lifted his feet off the staircase and slid away from the edge of the hole. Angelica's face rose from the hole and she looked around her, then did the same, followed by Hanna and Sue.

This room was just an old wooden floor with whitewashed walls. There was a short closed door in one wall. The staircase went the lengths of two men up again into another hole in the ceiling.

"Turn off your lights, so no one following can see us!" They did so and sat in utter darkness. Hanna peeked down into the staircase opening.

"I don't see anything at all. Everybody shush, listen." They all sat silent in darkness. It felt like forever. They heard nothing.

Sue had a coughing fit, from the dust or maybe nerves. The more she tried to stop, it only made the tickle worse.

Angelica hazarded the light, and crawled over to the door. She stood up and tried to open it. It worked. She quickly shone her light in. It was like a little corridor to another closed door. Jacky came up behind her. "Do we try it? or go up some more?"

Hanna came over. "Maybe up is out. It is kind of like the fire escape, it's metal. But Sue is still coughing, let's move fast. Sue! In here!"

Sue got up and joined them, and Hanna closed the door behind them. Jacky turned the knob on the second door, and it worked. He opened it a crack and listened and peered in. They were in darkness in the corridor, but there seemed a weird night light coming in, like from a window, the way a town is never really, really dark at night. Star viewing was always ruined by the light pollution. Sue had stopped coughing with the surprise of scrambling into this new mysterious place.

The room appeared to be empty so they crept inside and quietly closed the door behind them. It was a small room, furnished with two chairs, a small table, a very old rug, and—a fireplace to the right of the door they exited from, with a fire burning! They jumped as a log fell in and crackled in the fire. An open doorway without a door stood on the far side of the room, softly lit. Piles of books stood along the walls, and a spinning wheel. On the table appeared the remains of a meal, or someone had been interrupted before finishing. A metal cup, plate, and half a roll of bread. Some chicken bones picked totally clean.

Angelica snapped pictures. "Ghosts don't eat, or need fires, I would imagine. Unless that's an illusion created just for us."

They heard a giggle from the doorway. Hanna looked at them and then walked fearlessly to the door. She looked, then turned and waved them over.

There were real stairs here, which led down to a blank wall, just like the stairs leading up to the blank wall in the library. The stairs also went up, to a landing at a large window.

Sitting on the stairs looking down at them was a girl.

Chapter 28

Nocturnal

M eanwhile, Doreen was watching the library from the car. The rain had stopped. Joella was stretched out in the back seat. Rowan sat up front humming a peculiar tune. She was very still, not fidgety at all, and sat up very straight. Her eyes were closed.

Doreen saw a small black shadow run between the shrubs at the back wall of the library. Cat? Skunk? She watched the fire escape for any movement. The sky lit up; lightning flashed and lit the clouds, so that for a moment the scene looked like broad daylight.

Suddenly a hunched dark shadow figure with a pointed hat hurried across the garden. It seemed to come directly toward them. The dimly seen animal shot past out of the figure's shadow and disappeared in the dark. The pointy human sized figure was on the sidewalk right next to their car. Doreen clicked the locks which sounded very loud. Joella sat up. The figure passed into the puddle of light from the street lamp and turned to look at her through the window.

"It's a witch!" Joella yelled. The figure was a wretched old woman, wearing a black hooded cape. Her mouth hung open in a grimace and her lips curled back as if she were gasping for air through her mouth while she smelled something bad. She looked like the mask of a Greek tragedy. A front tooth was missing. She pulled her hood down over her forehead, dropped a bundle she had carried under her cloak, and hobbled away from them as fast as she could hobble.

Rowan said, "She's my mother."

Joella gaped. Doreen took a step forward.

"Don't follow her. She is frightened of people."

"What was she doing climbing the side of the library?" Doreen looked confounded, as she stopped to pick up the bundle.

"I don't know... She only comes out at night. She is just—afraid, to leave home and see people. That is just how she is. But I heard her voice in the library, in the poetry room. I couldn't believe it."

"And everyone thought you didn't even have a mother! Maybe she's a vampire..." Joella looked embarrassed when she blurted this out. She didn't want to offend Rowan.

Rowan shook her head. "She doesn't hurt anyone. She likes to help people. She is just...nervous about people. I don't know why. People are how they are. She's not a bad person. She's not even a bad mother."

Doreen smiled sympathetically at Rowan, handed over the bundle to her, then turned back to look at the library. "Well. Where do you suppose they are, already? Should we go back in?"

"The doors will be locked. How do we get back in, until they come out? Unless..." Rowan thought a minute. She opened the bundle of cloths tied together to reveal a small basket, with a couple books, some chicken bones in some crumpled wax paper. She set it down next to the car.

Joella jumped up and down. "We can climb up the fire escape!" Rowan and Doreen looked at her.

Doreen said, "No way. Too dangerous. And how do we know there's a way in when we get up there?"

"If my mother could climb it—who knows why, but it sure looked like that—then I can do it. I'll try. Maybe I can at least see what's going on inside, somewhere."

Doreen hesitated, nodded, and led Joella back to the car. "Be careful. I'll watch and listen from the car." She picked up the basket of cloths from where Rowan had left it on the sidewalk, and put it in on the floor in the front seat. Joella turned from the car with both hands on the window, watching Rowan.

Rowan closed her eyes, breathed deeply and opened her eyes, looking very still. Then she strode to the fire escape ladder and started the climb up the building.

Chapter 29

Lightfoot

I nside the newly discovered, secret rooms of the library, The Freep colleagues stared. The girl on the stairs was almost a woman. Probably once upon a time she would have been considered one. She looked the age of Angelica's big sisters; she looked, actually, like she could be Rowan's older sister, maybe in high school.

Except she was a mess. Her hair was very long and messy. Her dress was old, worn and dirty. She was barefoot. "I'm not a ghost," she said.

They stood and stared, and she stood up and walked past them back into the room. She ignored them while she took her seat at the table and looked at her unfinished meal. "I don't have much here. Would you like to share?"

She offered her metal cup around. They all shook their heads. Then she fiddled with some chicken bones on the table.

"Who are you?" Sue came closer to the table.

"May I take your picture?" The girl shook her head no, and Angelica put the phone down.

The strange girl toyed some more with the chicken bones on the table, arranging them in patterns, studying them. She then nodded, and looked up at the others. "What do you want to know? My name is Mary Lightfoot. I live here."

"In the library?" Hanna asked. "Why? Are you a prisoner?"

Sue said, "You're a Lightfoot? you own this place?" The rest looked at Sue in surprise. "Darn! I sent my backpack out with Joella. The scroll was a deed to a Lightfoot, I think?"

"Well. Currently I live here. Only for a little while. Only until I turn 18. I came to town last year to visit my aunt Acantha and cousin Rowan."

Just then they heard a hollow booming crash and the ringing of metal. Mary looked up. "Sounds like a visitor." She walked to a door they hadn't noticed behind bookshelves, and opened it to a bricked chimney room. On the floor crouched Rowan, dusty, wincing and rubbing her elbow.

"Hi. I figured out what that funnel chimney is for. I climbed up on the roof from the fire escape, heard voices in the funnel and slipped down into it. Hard landing here."

Rowan crawled out, stood and said, "Mary?"

Sue confronted Rowan. "Are you cousins? Why does your cousin live in the library?"

Rowan and Mary embraced and then turned and laughed at the rest of them.

"I'm not, technically, her cousin; Mary is my mother's niece, but I am really just a foster child."

"Like me! I have no parents either." Mary looked with delight at Rowan, while she spoke. "Rowan is a changeling! A fairy sprite!" She laughed. "Acantha took in Rowan when she was little, and has been her guardian since. Or, maybe Rowan has been Acantha's guardian." She laughed again.

"Wait. Is Acantha your mother's name? I saw that in the library meeting minutes, too. Isn't Acantha your, um, cat's name?" Sue looked at Rowan in confusion.

Rowan put her head back and laughed. "Well! You've heard me calling her, right?" Then she put an arm around Mary and said, "I use my mother's family name, Yazzie, in school, but I am no Lightfoot. Mary is. But Mary, I thought you had gone into the care system again, after your visit last year?"

Mary shook her head. "Acantha thought I would be in danger if I revealed myself locally. Minor descendants of Sam Lightfoot, who originally lived here, would get a life estate in the library. Acantha thought that the witches would kill me if they found me. They want to sell the library, which is very valuable. So I had to hide until I am 18, which is only a few months now. Acantha knew about the secret parts of the library. She had found them when she sneaks into the library at night to borrow books."

Rowan nodded slowly. "So she comes at night when no one is here, so she doesn't have to see or talk to anyone...I get it now."

Mary shrugged and laughed. "We thought it was funny that I am getting to live in the library as my ancestors intended! I had nowhere else to go. Acantha brings me what I need."

"Why don't you just, I don't know, sue them for your rights?" Sue opened her hands, palms up, puzzled.

"I don't care about the inheritance. It was more important to me to stay alive. I can live with Acantha and Rowan when it is safe."

Hanna said, "I totally get you. I wish I could live in the library."

Sue persisted. "Are you and Acantha the ones pretending to be a ghost downstairs? Writing on the mirror, and in the books and such?"

Mary looked at her strangely. "What? No. I don't go downstairs. I wouldn't write in a library book!"

"But who are the witches? Who would kill you?"

"I don't know. There is a coven who sneaks in and meets here. Haven't you seen their brooms and shovels about? I think they want the library for themselves. They sure don't want me to have it."

Chapter 30

Bones

"Doreen must be beside herself. We should go home now. Or at least, get them back in here." Angelica was pacing a little during this meeting with Mary, or following Jacky around as he wandered around the room looking up and down, and up the chimney in the little closet. Jacky returned to the table and was about to touch the chicken bones.

"Don't touch those! I'm using that," Mary called out.

Rowan looked at the others and explained, "Bones, and birds, are things of divination. Messages about the future. Ever make a wish on a wishbone?"

Sue muttered, "Iron and bone..."

Jacky took the rusty old iron key out of his pocket and tossed it on the table with the chicken bones. "Why is this key to the secret upstairs concealed in the reading room fireplace, if Acantha has been coming in through the chimney?"

"Also, I cannot believe my mother comes down that chimney! She'd have to use magic not to get hurt by that! And how would she get out, but through the library?"

"No, there's another way in. They never come up here to lock the old doors and windows. Look, at the window seat in the stairwell, that old door never really fully closes shut, I let Acantha in there. The fire steps have a landing there."

"How do we get back downstairs to let in Doreen and Joella? Or do we just leave from here?"

"Don't forget, someone was down there. Talking. Following us."

"What if they look out the window and see us climbing down on the fire ladder?"

Sue tapped on her teeth with a thumbnail. "Anybody remember exactly how to get out of here?"

Jacky said, "I can do it! Through that door, down the metal spiral staircase, down again, through the cellar...I can scout if you like? If it's clear, I can scoot out and tell Doreen what is going on, and then come back for you."

Angelica took his hand and looked up at him. "She's my sister. I'll come."

Sue's eyes went from one to the other. "But I'll have to come with you. Joella..."

Rowan shook her head. "I would go, alone! But I didn't come that way and don't know it. I'll watch from here. If anything goes wrong, Mary can let me out here and I'll climb down out there."

Hanna settled into a chair by the fire. "We shouldn't be too big a group, to be more agile and less noticeable. I'll stay here with Mary. No one even knows I was at the library tonight, remember? I could stay indefinitely, and maybe I will."

There wasn't time to argue or think any of this through. Sue didn't want to go down there again, but she was uncomfortable with the long separation from her little sister. "I'll just go."

"And me." Angelica dropped Jacky's hand and stood close by Sue. "Jacky, we're smaller and—quieter..."

"Ok, well, I want to climb down the fire escape anyway, so I'll wait." Jacky took a post by Rowan at the window.

Mary pleaded, "Just don't tell anyone about me up here! Please!"

Sue put her fingers to her lips in a shushing sign and set off with Angelica to retrace their steps.

It took time for their eyes to adjust in the darkness. Then Angelica remembered. She whispered, "Just don't cough, Sue!"

Of course saying that was the wrong thing. The anxiety of stifling a cough immediately set in and tickled. They decided to press through fast, as they didn't hear or see anything below. Angelica would take a quick look with her phone light before they descended, then shut it off. Angelica descended the twisting metal staircase first and Sue felt for each step with her feet.

In this way they made it all the way to the ground level again, the dirt floor. There was the door hanging open, stuck on the uneven floor. They listened to nothing. Maybe an acorn rolling in the ductwork now and then. All cellars sounded like that. Angelica flashed her light onto the floor and even took a picture of the uneven floor wedging the door open. Then they scurried through the dark basement, around the table of books toward the dim light at the cellar door. They looked up the stairs. Saw nothing. Absolutely nothing. The shovel they had seen before was gone.

Chapter 31

Police

Here on the stairs the two of them could fit together and they crept up each step together, out of fairness; otherwise, it was just too scary for the first one in line. They got up the short staircase to the emergency exit landing and looked up the stairs, seeing no one in the dim red exit sign light.

Angelica whispered, "Ok, now who stays here to hold the door open, and who runs out to the car to report?"

Sue looked a little sick. "And then one is left to go back up to tell the others to come out? Or am I to come back in with them, or alone?"

Angelica whispered furiously, "I'm going out, to talk to my sister. If you go, Joella will never let you come back here." Sue knew that for certain too. "I'll be right back. There's a little light here from the exit sign. Wait right here, keep the door open a crack and watch."

Sue nodded, feeling sicker. Angelica pushed the door out a tiny bit and instantly pulled it shut again.

"Oh, great. There are police officers walking right by. They'll see us, sneaking out of the library at this hour!"

"Maybe we can get to another door. One near a window so we can watch and time it." They proceeded two together up the stairs to the staff room door at the top of the staircase. Angelica put her ear to the door to the staff kitchenette. She shook her head. She pushed the door open a tiny bit and held the flashlight up ahead as they snuck into the kitchen and silently, slowly, opened the door to the poetry room. The little battery candle was still lit on the table. They went in and quickly and quietly closed the door and paused there.

They looked at each other in horror. The women's voices were there in the room with them, again!

Has any new evidence been found?

No! We feel sure there was another deed, eliminating the Lightfoot rights. We dug

under the floor and in the garden. We found
a lot of old trash but nothing helpful.

Does it matter? I mean, who is there, to object?

The girls stared at each other and then looked wildly around the room and down the hall. Sue's eyes widened and she pointed up. Angelica looked up at a vent in the ceiling. Sue coughed. They froze. No voices.

Angelica tiptoed into the hallway and Sue followed. "The voices are up," Angelica pointed to the ceiling as she whispered into Sue's ear. "Let's go down. And get out of here."

It was darker once the stair turned, the further down they got from the battery candle in the poetry room. Sue was used to adjusting to night sight because of her star gazing, but Angelica felt nervous without her flashlight. They sat on a stair and started sliding down each step on their bottoms, so they wouldn't trip and fall. It was slow but quiet and safe. At the first floor, they stared into the darkness in both directions, and listened. Dark, and quiet.

They had two options out now. The front door, on Main Street; someone was sure to see them, there would be people walking or lingering on the sidewalks after bar visits. The back door, where they could peek out the window in the children's room, and then exit right to where Doreen was parked on the side street.

They tiptoed to the main desk. Light came in from a skylight over the back door, the light from the garden lamppost.

The door to the children's room was shut.

Chapter 32

Coven

The girls needed to see out the window in the children's room to know if they would be able to leave the library unseen by witnesses, especially the police. So Angelica looked at Sue and pressed her ear against the door. She looked at Sue and shook her head. Nothing could be heard through the door. She put her hand on the doorknob. Sue cringed. Angelica huddled close to the door and Sue leaned in over her head. Angelica very carefully, very slowly, turned the doorknob. She was able to open it the barest crack. The room was dimly lit. They each put an eye to the crack in the door.

Present around the children's desk in front of the sealed fireplace were Ms. Wanda, Ms. Kaycee and the man who had watched from the car! Sue inhaled her breath, Angelica waved her silent.

The grownups were all dressed in black. The room smelled of smoke, in that way it had; no one appeared to be smoking. On an open area of the floor was spread a plastic tablecloth on which were clumps of dirt and clay, and old broken objects, ceramics, rusty tools. Around the tarp lay dirty brooms.

The people were talking in ordinary voices, evidently unaware of the children's presence in the library. Sue looked up and spied a vent above the desk. The voices in Poetry had come from here?

"Well, another useless night. I know my great-grandmother said there was a later transaction where the Lightfoot life tenant sold his rights, and a new Deed was made. I would have thought it was somewhere in or around this building," Ms. Wanda scowled.

"What do we care, though? Who would come forward to stop the sale?" Ms. Kaycee looked tired and irritated.

"What about that Yazzie kid. Other side's Lightfoot, right?" The man crouched next to the tablecloth and pocketed something shiny.

"Worse case, we report her mother for neglect. The girl is completely unsupervised, lives alone. Put her into care.

She'll be in a home in the south counties. No one will be speaking for her." Wanda cackled. "Did the kids scare off, do you think?"

Kaycee giggled. "Sure. And they'll be spreading the word in the school newspaper. When school reopens. You know, we could probably close for awhile. That would help fuel the rumors, and seem to make the haunting stories true, and seem to excuse our closing. Especially after the threatening messages. It could be put out there that vandalism at the library is being investigated..."

Wanda nodded. "Officer Sykes could recommend closing the library for safety until the investigation is completed."

"Vicious circle," the man chuckled, rubbing his hands together and standing up. "Desicco Construction can't wait to build that tower of luxury apartments, parking deck and office/warehouse complex."

"Sal, we're not going to actually destroy this old building, though?" Ms. Kaycee asked for confirmation.

"Nah. Rental office. Way to promote during County History Weekend."

The man turned around and wandered around the room, as Sue teetered, leaning on Angelica who accidentally pushed the door a little. It squeaked. The man looked up sharply, narrowed his eyes and took large strides toward them.

The two girls slammed the door shut. Sue felt so scared she couldn't breathe. But she looked at Angelica and pointed to the back door. They took the chance. Sue opened the door and they both ran. They had to run down and around the long ramp, between the railings which felt like a cage right now. Sue looked back. The man opened the door and stood in the doorway, watching them flee. He leaned against the door, gave out a belly laugh, and turned back inside, pulling the door shut. And locked.

The girls skittered to the corner. Fortunately no one seemed to be in the back garden to see them exit the library. Unfortunately, Doreen's car was gone.

Chapter 33

Search Party

"**H**oly! Doreen's leaving!" Jacky spun around from the window.

"Where are Sue and Angelica?" Hanna asked him, without getting up from her seat by the fire.

"Well. Someone will have to find them and tell them, if they're still in here. And someone will need to let them back in, if they are outside. Wait, they weren't with Doreen already, were they? I didn't see them come outside, did you, Jacky?"

"Nope. I didn't see them cross to where the car was parked. I can't see straight down the building from in here though." He started to unfasten the window and fold it out to lean out over the metal stair, then started to put a leg out over the window casement to go down himself.

"Wait! Someone will still have to let you all back inside! We will have to go down anyway. I don't know the way you guys came in..."

Hanna got up. "I can go down with you."

Mary was scrutinizing the chicken bones. She shook her head. "I don't think you should all go. What if they ran into someone down there, and are being held? What if you all end up captured? Who will get help?"

Jacky said, "What if someone—or something—has them! I better come!"

Mary startled them with her own offer. "OK, you all go. I'll keep watching for now. If I see you or them, I'll flag you. If nothing ever happens, I'll climb down myself, and look in the windows. And get Acantha."

Rowan looked doubtful, and was torn between where she was most needed. Jacky looked like he wasn't sure Mary could be counted on. He grabbed up the iron key, just in case they had to get back up here, and pushed it into Hanna's hand. Hanna led the way back out, down, and down again, in the dark, and Rowan followed silently. Behind her Jacky took one more look at Mary, signed a salute, and brought up the rear.

In the dark cellar they stopped again and listened. The door remained jammed open on the dirt and sand floor, which had plainly shifted somehow at some time. When they reached the back stair emergency exit, Jacky pushed the door open to look. No one was around. So they concluded they would have to search the rest of the library for Sue and Angelica.

They crept back up, through the staff kitchen to the poetry room, stopping to listen closely at each point. In the poetry room, where they had last heard voices, there was only silence. Jacky mimed getting the key back from Hanna, who raised her eyebrows, got it from her pocket and handed it over. Jacky returned the key to behind the loose brick where he had found it. "In case," he whispered. "For safekeeping." He looked a little grim, for Jacky.

They listened at the top of the stairs. Their eyes stared down into the blackness below. Dark silence. Rowan reached out her hands, palms up. "I'll go first. I can see in the dark." She went so lightly before them that they were afraid they had lost her. Then Hanna bumped into her. Hanna put a hand on Rowan's shoulder, and Jacky put a hand on Hanna's, and they felt in the dark with the toes of their sneakers for each next step.

"Jacky is going to fall on us and we're all tumbling down the stairs," hissed Hanna. "Jacky, use your darn flashlight, just keep the spotlight down on the stair, don't wave it around." He flicked it on and they proceeded.

On the first floor, there was enough light coming in the windows from streetlights outside that they could peer around the corner into the main checkout area. Nothing. No sound. The door to the children's room was open as usual and showed only darkness. Rowan crept down into the room and stopped, sniffing.

"What?" Hanna followed her.

"I'm not sure..."

"Look!" Jacky waved them over. He had opened the back door. "There they are!"

Chapter 34

Stuck on the Stage

R owan and Hanna stood at the door to the library, holding it open, and Jacky flew out to tackle Angelica and Sue in a hug. Sue almost wept with relief to see him.

"They're gone!"

"I know."

"We didn't know what to do," Angelica told Jacky. "We narrowly escaped capture by the people meeting in the children's room. We risked running right into the police, but they were gone. Doreen's gone."

Sue cut in. "We considered going to my house as the closest, but how do we explain where Joella is?"

"Same, if we showed up at my house without Doreen." Angelica stepped a little closer to Jacky and crossed her arms, rubbing them warm.

"Maybe Rowan would take us home?" Sue looked hopeful. "Joella might think of looking for us at Rowan's house?"

"What people? What police? There's no one in the children's room," Jacky shook his head like a dog clearing out his ears, and looked at the girls, puzzled. "Look, there's Rowan and Hanna waiting for you. I can't think what to do about Doreen and Joella driving off without us, though."

As they looked at the door to the library, it suddenly shut. They looked at each other. Jacky laughed. He ran to the back door and pounded. The two girls shrugged, took his word for it that the coven had gone, and joined him.

"Open up, guys. We need to decide what to do next."

The door opened. The big man reached out and grabbed the three of them in a bear hug, and maneuvered them into the door and shut it. Jacky started punching his back, as the man threw the two girls down the short steps into the children's room. He turned around and belted Jacky across his head, who stumbled. The man picked him up and threw him down the stairs on top of the girls. "Ya wanted to spend the night in the library?

Enjoy! You're in trouble tomorrow! I'm just 'security'!"
The man laughed and slammed the youth room door
shut from outside. The children scrambled up, ran to
the door and tried to open it, but it wouldn't budge.
Angelica flicked on the light switch. Sue shook her head
and flipped it off again.

They turned around. By the dim light filtering in the
windows from the garden lamppost, they saw Rowan
and Hanna sitting next to each other on a bench seat
inside the little stage coach replica. This was a fixture in
the room for children to sit in and play in. The girls were
leaning forward; their hands were tied to a broomstick
which was stuck on the outside of the stagecoach across
the two "window" openings, and they couldn't have
got out, at least not quickly enough to help rescue the
newcomers. Otherwise they did not appear to be injured.
Neither Rowan nor Hanna were crying. They looked
stoic, with chins jutting out and defiant eyes.

Angelica took her phone out of her back pocket and
snapped a photo, with the flash. Sue went to Ms. Kaycee's
desk and rummaged for a scissors, while Jacky tried to
work the broom handle out of the tie loops.

Sue cut the ties. She put her finger on her lips and
pointed over her head to the vent in the ceiling over
the desk. "We need to plan quietly, in case someone is

listening," she whispered. "Also we should keep listening, in case we can hear them."

Hanna and Rowan climbed out of the stage coach, stood up, stretched and rubbed their wrists. Rowan went to watch at the window. She tried the window lock and sash but the multi-paned windows were fixed and painted shut, and the windows on this first level were barred, anyway. Hanna listened at the door. "There's a keyhole here," she showed Sue. "I never noticed how the door locks from the other side, but...?" Sue nodded, and went to empty the desk drawer onto the desk and sift through the contents. Jacky checked the interior of the fireplace and was feeling around the bricks surrounding the fireplace hearth. Angelica joined him. They were searching for, hoping for, another key.

Chapter 35

Trunk

R owan turned from the window to stare at the stage coach. In front of the stage was a chest. She squinted at it. "What is that?" She pointed.

Sue looked up. "Oh. That chest. It's locked. It's been locked as long as we have been coming here. All the kids always want to know what's in it. The librarians never knew, and said they had no key for it. We used to pretend. Toys. Treasure. Weapons. A skeleton. Probably empty!"

"Why is it locked?"

"I don't know. I always figured, so the kids wouldn't climb into it, or slam the top on their fingers."

Angelica crawled out from the hearth, filthy with dirt. "Look." She held up a tiny blackened key, like the key that fit into Joella's ballerina jewel box at home. Like a diary key. "It was in that old cauldron in the fireplace."

Hanna snatched it from her and strode to the door. "It doesn't do anything. It's so tiny, I'm afraid of losing it in the door!"

Rowan walked over to the trunk in front of the stage. She knelt down. "It's a tiny padlock." She looked at Hanna. Hanna came over and offered the key.

Jacky grinned. "I can't believe that tonight, we are finally going to find out what's in that box. It's like, the night to end all secrets, or something."

"I only wish Joella were here, she was obsessed with that trunk." Sue shook her head, eyes wide. "Wait until I tell her that Ms. Kaycee is in on it all. She'll be heartbroken."

Jacky and Hanna looked at her. "What?" Sue just shrugged and waved her hand. She was getting really tired, too tired.

Rowan looked at the key, and at the tiny padlock. Angelica knelt and shone her phone's flashlight on it. Rowan fitted the key to the padlock, wiggled it, turned it. With the other hand she pulled on it. The shackle opened.

Rowan slipped out the lock. Everyone crowded around, and Rowan lifted the top.

Sue sneezed, and a puff of dust rose from the trunk.

It seemed to be empty. It was deeper than it looked, and black inside. Deeper than the carpeted floor.

Jacky shown a light into it. There was no floor. The trunk was just a hole in the bottom. Jacky pulled a coin out of his pocket and threw it in with a little force. "Make a wish." It bounced down and down. They peered down. Yes, there were steps there! Barely. More like ladder rungs.

"Creepy!"

"Is it a well?"

Rowan said, "Probably more like a cellar, the way to a root cellar, or storm cellar, or something. Or maybe, a passage? A way out?" Rowan's hair was shining weirdly in the oblong of striped light coming from the window. "I'll go down. Watch from the top, I'll keep you posted. Someone stay at the window, too." Hanna went to the window but half turned to watch them at the trunk as well. Jacky handed down his flashlight to Rowan.

Sue wouldn't have thought Rowan could fit down there, but down she went. Angelica pointed her phone light down. They could see the top of Rowan's head descending. A ways down, she jumped off the ladder and was on a floor. They saw the dim flashlight beam swished around.

"I think it was just another way down to the same cellar. It's the same place, it comes out behind the furnace; we didn't notice the ladder on the wall before. We could get out through the emergency exit, or go up into the library again, or go up to Mary."

"Mary!" Hanna screamed. Something had fallen past the window outside and landed in the shrubs under the window. An animal yowled. They heard Mary cry out in pain.

Chapter 36

Rescue

"Let's go down and get out of here! We have to help Mary." Hanna stepped into the trunk and started climbing down. Rowan was holding the dim flashlight on the bottom of the ladder. Sue climbed in next and gingerly felt for the first rung. Her hands were sweating. She rubbed her eyes on one arm to get the itchy hair out of her face and stepped down. When they were down, Jacky followed, then Angelica, with her phone propped in her waistband with the light on.

Rowan grabbed a few books off the table and ran. They followed her up out of the basement, up the stairs to the emergency exit. She opened it and they all fled; Rowan wedged the pile of books between the door and library wall, so they could get back immediately if necessary, and ran to Mary.

Mary was badly scraped and scratched but she seemed whole. Jacky grabbed her hands and helped her up out of the shrubbery. "I didn't fall far, nothing broken! It was just sharp!" She laughed. "I don't know. I was worried about you, I was going to go get help from Acantha. Then I stepped on something alive, an animal, instead of a step, and freaked out, and fell!"

At that moment they saw a car's headlights approaching. "Oh, no. Quick, hide yourselves," Hanna scolded, and scrunched herself behind the shrubs against the brick wall of the library. Mary, Sue, Angelica and Jacky did the same. Rowan stayed standing still as could be and watched the car. It pulled up on the side street under the street light. It was Doreen. She and Joella waved madly at them through the windshield.

They all ran for the car and piled in. "Where did you go?" Angelica cried.

"The police were walking over. I couldn't decide whether to ask them for help for you guys, since I didn't know what was happening in there for so long. But I also didn't want everyone to get in trouble. So I just left!"

"We've been driving around," pouted Joella.

"I told you, I think best when I'm driving." Doreen smiled. "Where to?"

"Sleepover at home, I think. We have that big sleeping porch, you can all stay."

"Man, Harry doesn't know what he's missing," Jacky spread out both arms along the back seat.

"Mary and I can walk home from here, we'll be fine. Mom can help fix Mary up." Rowan and Mary started up the sidewalk.

"Can you just drop us home, Doreen? Probably OK to go home at this point."

"Yeah, if mom asks, Doreen brought us home! Because I couldn't sleep!" Joella crossed her arms.

Doreen drove around the block to make sure Rowan and Mary were just about home, and waved.

Everybody was soon where they were going to spend the night. Jacky was asleep on the porch almost instantly, even before Angelica threw a sleeping bag at him. Hanna shared Angelica's room. Doreen told them all to sleep on it for now and they would catch each other up in the morning.

At home, Sue resolved to talk to Harry about all this tomorrow. And her parents. And then write all this up for publication in *The Freep.* She would understand it all better once she saw it written down, and could think about it.

Dog whined to join her, and snuggled up in Sue's bed with her. Then Joella climbed in. They heard Georgie reciting rhymes to himself across the hall. They heard their father's snores from down the hall, right through the walls.

Yes, she would work this out with Harry's help tomorrow. She didn't think, though, they would meet at the library.

Chapter 37

Spinning

S ue and Joella slept late of course. When they were at the table for lunch, Joella complained of a headache. Mom was sympathetic, but brisk. She wasn't fond of sleepovers, and encouraged the girls to choose alternative arrangements—to stay home, to host. The girls' exhaustion was a consequence to be borne. Education is expensive.

"I know you're tired from being up all night, but do you know what? Exercise wouldn't hurt. Help you get to bed early tonight. Why don't you take Dog for a walk, and Georgie; they really missed you."

Sue groaned, Joella whined, Georgie screamed. Mom laughed. When they finished their scrambled eggs, Mom handed Sue the leash.

"Mom, I need to call Harry first, OK? Maybe he can come with us."

"A walk-and-talk! That's a fine idea. And we're looking forward to hearing about your evening when you feel restored." Mom bustled off. Joella slumped onto the couch, feet up, pillow over her head. Georgie squeezed in and sprawled on top of her, head on top the pillow.

Harry wasn't even up yet when she called, and he had gone home—sure, at a late hour, but at least it was before this morning. He came to the phone and from his voice she could imagine him all droopy eyed and groggy with his hair sticking up.

"Harry, you missed your Saturday morning tutoring?" Harry tutored other kids at the Cultural Center. He was very sought after; it was funny to see the parents clamoring to speak with him for his opinion on their children. Sue wondered at them; Harry was himself just a child, after all. How had he acquired this authority with adults?

"No, I had canceled it, because of our thing. Ready to fill me in? Let me just do my morning ablutions and call you back."

"Morning oblations?"

Harry laughed. "Well, yes, that too." Sue waited, a question mark between them. "Ablutions means, washing up. Oblations is like, an offering to God. You're right, you reminded me to do both! I'll call you."

"Wait. I have to walk the dog and my siblings. We can come by. Look for me on the sidewalk and join us? Talk then?"

It was arranged. Then Joella suggested putting Georgie or Dog in her old doll carriage. Then Joella asked if Sue would push her in the baby carriage. Sue shook her head and said, "Hold Georgie's hand, or take the leash. Which?"

Joella suggested the shoulder harness leash for Georgie, and he was all in to play dog, or pony cart.

"Georgie, you're almost old enough that that is just weird. I don't really want to be seen in that scene," and Sue put her foot down. Finally they were on their way. Usually Joella would be dragging Georgie along because he stopped every few inches to look at something, but today since she was so tired, she was almost sleep walking, and just yawned and tarried with him as needed. Sue and Dog tried to follow them, to keep their eyes on the littler ones moseying ahead.

Harry was standing on the sidewalk in front of his building, all slicked and neat and pressed. He smiled broadly at their little parade and fell in with Sue. Harry and Sue tried to slow their steps a bit to let the younger ones plus animal get a little distance ahead, but Dog kept planting it and turning back to look for Sue. So they walked all the way to the turn off to the playground, while Sue tried to fill in the missing details for Harry, and for Joella, as it turned out after all. Joella was too tired to do her usual climbing so the three of them sat on the swings while Dog chased Georgie as he went around on the spinner. The silent large rectangle blank of the covered swimming pool in the middle of the playground reminded Sue bleakly of endings, like a grave for the innocent summer screams and joyful splashing of the neighborhood. A sudden gust swirled dried leaves into a kid sized cyclone, and dropped the rubbish as suddenly onto the white cover.

"So what should we do? I mean, are we even safe at the library? What do we do when we see Ms. Kaycee around? Are we safe anywhere?"

Chapter 38

Off Leash

Harry couldn't even believe how much he'd missed. About Ms. Kaycee's being in with Ms. Wanda on the scheme to scare people away from the library, and the thug and their imprisonment in the children's room, about Mary Lightfoot's secret residence in the library; and how Rowan seemed to have solved the ghost woman as movie, but there was still a lot of unexplained evidence.

"We could go check on Mary. I'll take you to Rowan's," Sue offered.

Joella jumped up. "I'm ready. Let's go, Georgie-Porgie!" Dog and Georgie raced each other to the swings, and she knelt and restored Dog's collar.

They took the south street which would cross the main street, Post Road, by the library and take them up to Rowan's block on Bank Street. The library would be closed by now, but after last night, they no longer took comfort in its public closing time. The bright sun today, a shopping day, made them feel braver about walking past the building. People were lingering at sidewalk tables over espresso or ice cream. Truly, walking had given the girls a second wind, or maybe it was the breeze at their backs pushing them on to keep up with Harry's crisp footsteps. Georgie seemed rested and refreshed from their stop at the play yard. "I want ice cream."

"We'll get some on the way back, to bring home, Georgie." They were on the sidewalk which passed the library on the east side and which would take them to the garden memorial yard. The building cast a dark shadow over the sidewalk and they would have to walk through it. The window in the reading room, where the glass case had been (and the reflection of the woman in yellow) loomed on this side. Joella, Georgie and Dog trotted ahead. Sue walked quickly past the building without looking up, chatting bravely with Harry about whether, and how, to lay out their story in *The Freep*. They stepped past the corner of the building and started the uphill climb, passing by the garden.

Suddenly a black animal streaked past them, and Dog slipped her collar and took off after. The children turned in dismay, shouting, "Shea!" They ran after and saw the dark animal streak into the library emergency exit, where Rowan had propped the door open with books last night. Dog followed it right in.

"Oh no! Now we have to get them out, and close that door!" Harry nodded grimly, took a deep breath and stood tall. He pulled the door open wider and held it for them. Sue picked up Georgie and stepped into the library with Joella; Harry stepped in, removed the books from the floor, and shut the door.

"Now what?" They all stood on the landing. They didn't see the animals, but Dog was barking on the upstairs landing at the kitchenette door. The air in the stairwell felt icy cold, unlike the sun-warmed sidewalk outside.

"She might be barking at us. She can get up the stairs, but sometimes she's afraid to come down a long steep flight."

"I want to see the poetry room, the words on the mirror," Harry said.

"Come on, Georgie, we're in the library and there's no one else here!" Joella started to scramble up the stairs and Georgie clapped his hands.

"Shh!" Sue shushed everyone. "This may not be safe. We need to get Shea and get out of here. Joella, get back down here. Sit right here on the step and hold Georgie's hand. Ice cream for everyone when we get out. Meanwhile, don't move!" Georgie bumped down the few steps at the bottom and then climbed up and repeated his trick, and made Joella giggle.

Sue turned and frowned at them as she and Harry crept up the stairs. Dog had stopped barking in favor of madly wagging his whole self. Sue grabbed him up and Harry pushed open the upstairs door a bit. Lights were off, no sound; after-hours feel. "I'm just gonna look, quick," he said, and disappeared into the staff room.

Chapter 39

Scraps

S ue maneuvered Shea down the stairs, where the dog enjoyed a joyous reunion with Georgie and Joella. In just a moment the door at the top of the stairs opened again and Harry stepped out. "Hold open the exit door," he called down softly. Sue looked surprised. She made sure Dog was on leash again and instructed Joella to hold the animal tightly in her arms, and Sue opened the door and stood against it to hold it open. Harry hissed "shoo" and the shadow cat flew down the stairs and out the door, startling Georgie terribly, who started to cry. He had, after all, just undergone rabies shot treatment for tangling with this or some similar creature.

Harry jogged down the stairs and motioned them all outside. Sue looked both ways out the door and saw no one, so they all tumbled out, closing the door carefully and running up the street to the corner with Bank. They stopped there under a huge tree. "I'm tired," came pitifully from Georgie.

"You're tired?" Joella said, hands on hips. "I was up all night." Sue gave Georgie and Joella each a big hug.

Harry held out an envelope to Sue. "Look at this." Sue took it and pulled out a ragged scrap of paper, on which were ink stamped the words, BOOK 2A PAGE 159. She looked at Harry, puzzled. "I don't know," he said. "But that cat had it. I looked in the poetry room. The mirror was still marked up, by the way. And the cat jumped out of one of the bookshelves, and a book fell down, and the cat had this in its teeth. It dropped the paper on my feet, and walked over and waited at the door.

"I picked up the book, it was that nursery rhyme book; it didn't look ripped or anything. I don't know which book had the envelope in it, or where the scrap is ripped from."

"I think Acantha is just helping you. I think it's a clue," Joella said, having been listening intently.

"I'm tired," whined Georgie. "I want ice cream."

"Okay. Well it's a long walk back at this point. How about we rest a little at Rowan's house?"

"Yes, yes!" Joella jumped up and down, so Georgie followed suit. Sue pocketed the envelope for consideration later.

As they climbed the stone steps in the hill to Rowan's place, they heard Rowan and Mary laughing in the garden; both were delighted at the company. Sue introduced Harry and Georgie, who asked for ice cream. "I don't think we have any of that, but I have something you will like better." Sue, Harry and Joella took the three seats at the table and Georgie sat on the story stump. Rowan said not a word, but went with Mary inside and returned with a plate with a towel over it. Mary held plates and utensils, and Rowan dished out squares of a soft, yellow, custard-like cake with spices sprinkled on top. Georgie was humming to himself on the stump.

"I know you," Georgie said. "You're the girl in the library," he spoke to Mary. Mary looked surprised.

"I didn't think we'd met?"

"I dreamed it. There's another girl who lives in the library, too. I've seen her when I was there for a puppet show. She hides in the chimneys."

Sue shivered. He had picked up more info than she'd thought, when she and Harry were talking. "Don't mind him. He thinks his teachers live at school, too." Georgie glared at her, but Rowan brought him a serving of the creamy yellow dessert. He tried it and closed his eyes, making "mmm" noises.

"I don't suppose any of you know what this might mean. We found it at the library," Sue passed around the scrap of paper, as they all shook their heads. "Do you think I could ask Acantha?"

Rowan looked at her as she picked up the empty plates, and spoke deliberately. "Acantha is not available right now."

Chapter 40

Hall of Records

T he little party at Rowan's suddenly felt awkward. None of them had had enough sleep, and the sweet had made everyone feel drowsy. Dog woke up from his nap on Sue's feet, and their little group took their leave and headed down the hill, while Rowan and Mary packed up their tea time and went banging through the screen door.

"I know ice cream was promised, but we're full now, right?" Georgie nodded as he trudged down Bank Street between Sue and Harry.

Joella had Dog. "Sue. Do you think that was Acantha?"

"The cat? Maybe. She wasn't at Rowan's."

"I mean, is the cat, her mother? They have the same name. She wasn't there either."

Sue didn't answer. In truth, she didn't know what to say about that, even though the question hardly made sense.

Georgie said, "I have the same name as my father." They all walked in silence, wondering their own thoughts.

They reached Harry's turn-off. "I'll come with?"

"Sure," Sue assured him. They walked past Harry's turn and approached the little park at home, where a swan family was heading down the canal. Sue smiled, then followed Joella, Georgie and Dog as they loped up the porch and crashed their way into the kitchen/family room.

"Hi, Harry," Mom smiled as she filled Dog's dishes, to Shea's boundless appreciation. Joella and Georgie ran off upstairs.

"Hey, Mom!" Harry's hearty reply charmed mothers; his making himself at home as one of the family complimented their hospitality.

"Mom, we have so much going on," Sue said from the kitchen stool, as she helped herself to a carrot stick from a platter Mom placed before them.

"Tell." Mom sat down with them.

Sue sighed long and deeply to tell the story again. Her mother's attention was riveted on her when she got to the

Mary part. Harry ate veggies and watched them. When Sue got to the part about the three adults in the children's room, and what happened then, her mother called out, "George. Join us please. You should hear this."

Her father came up the cellar stairs, wiping his hands on a rag, and sat with them in the kitchen. Her mother quickly summarized what she'd heard while Sue poured glasses of water for herself and Harry, and coffee from the pot which was always on, for her parents. She caught them up to today. "I can't believe you pulled that, staying in the library," her father said first. Harry looked slightly panicked about being present for this.

"I know...it was for Hanna, at first. Then, I just wanted to know more. I couldn't stop."

"I'm going to call the library director over at the county," her mother concluded.

"Mom, they'll just be mad, and get us all in trouble!"

"Actually, do you know what this could mean? Sue, where's that paper." Harry tried changing the subject a little. Sue reached into her pocket and pulled out the envelope with the little scrap of old paper, with the Book and Page reference stamped on it.

Her parents passed it back and forth. "Well I don't know what this is, or why it's in the library, but that is the way important property documents are recorded," her father started. "If you like, you two can come with me to work tomorrow, and go to the Hall of Records. Deeds, mortgages, and other property documents were kept in big books. New ones can be found online; if this is "Book 2" somewhere, it probably goes way back. They have not all been digitized yet, and if this is a local reference, it may still be in an actual book."

"Can anyone look?" Harry asked.

Sue's mother explained that documents about the rights in a piece of property have to be recorded for the public to see. The public has to have notice of rights to a piece of property. Otherwise there would be no way to check what you are buying, for example, if someone else owned that lot. "The recording is sort of the most important part. It doesn't really count if a property transaction is not recorded. Because someone who gets the property later might get to keep it, if there was no notice of an earlier transfer of rights. We are allowed to rely on the notice given."

"So there can't be secret deals?" Sue asked.

"Not unless you want to buy a bridge I am selling," her father chuckled. "Why don't you come with me tomorrow to see for yourselves how it works? Do some investigation under our noses during public hours, instead of sneaking around."

Chapter 41
Quiet Title

"D o you think this could help Mary? or help the town keep the library?" Sue asked Harry on Monday, as they got out of her dad's car and walked into the old brick county courthouse building. Her father waved and drove off to park. They were to meet at his neighboring office when they were done. "My parents said there is a kind of court case a person can bring to have decided who really owns property and gets to keep it. It's called "quiet title".

"Ha. Maybe that's just what the restless spirits need, for the title to be quiet. Maybe quiet title would keep those developers away and leave the library and its ghosts in peace. I don't know how this will all work out for Mary.

"But it is cool to be able to write in *The Freep* that we did this research. Double duty for our town history project, too!

"Plus, I might want to be a lawyer. My parents are very glad of this opportunity. Can we watch your dad in court, too?"

"Neither of them has court today," Sue sighed. "He's just in his office. Lucky we don't have school. Feels like take your kid to work day. But you heard, right, that school will open again Wednesday?"

"Yes. My parents are so glad. Especially because the library is closed, too."

"Yeah, my mother called the library," (Sue winced), "and they were closed. Then she left a message for the Director at the county." Sue shrugged dispiritedly and sighed.

At the counter they showed the scrap of the deed book reference. The woman didn't think anything of the scrap of paper; probably most people just jotted down on some scrap what they wanted to see. Sue also gave the woman her father's business card. The woman looked at it, smiled, and led them to a table. "Wait here." She returned wearing a smock and a pair of gloves, and carrying a huge leather book with fading gold letters. She carefully turned to page 159.

They held their breaths hoping the page would match something.

"No, there's nothing here. The first page of the next document is at 164. The prior document begins at page 147." The children looked stunned. "Do you have the right town?" she asked them. Harry and Sue looked at each other. The woman studied the book. "You know, there do seem to be pages missing. There does seem to be a gap in the page numbering. The back binding is broken; pages may have been lost. We are talking, here, about the year 1780. Do you know the names of the parties you are looking for? You may find something in the index."

"Try Lightfoot," Harry suggested. The woman carefully turned the book over and lifted off the back cover, and checked the alphabetical listings. "Lightfoot, Tom, heir to Sagamore Sam Lightfoot Sprekenduch, from Hendrickson, Casper. Page 159! That's the missing one. There is no way to know from here what property was transferred, though. You want the services of a title searcher."

"Is there a way of getting copies of the property records pertaining to the Semblance Library?" Sue asked, as she wrote in her notebook.

"We are not permitted to perform searches for you, but you can search property records on the computer over there. Records on the computer go back to 1923. We are still working on transferring archival records from these books to the computer system. Some of the old books have been lost or destroyed, but we do have books which go back to 1748." The woman patted the book fondly in her glove, and picked it up, cradling the giant book in her arms. "We can charge print copies to your office, if you like, to take any documents you select with you." The woman looked at them over her glasses and smiled, and returned to the inner offices behind the glass windows at the counter.

Sue went to the computer table. Harry jiggled the mouse and Sue leaned over his shoulder to read the instructions. "You can search by the address. Forty-four Old Post Road." They selected every document which appeared in the search results, and clicked print. The sign over the computer said, "Pick up your documents at the Fee Register".

Soon they had rushed up to Dad's office with a yellow folder filled with papers and were ushered into a conference room, where they spread the papers out. The papers were stapled into separate multi-page documents. Harry spread them in date order from oldest on left; they looked at the first pages of the documents and Sue wrote a list in her notebook:

Proprietors, Black and Dun Inn, to Serg
Boogman, 1929

Serg Boogman to Bram Meyer, 1931

Estate of Meyer to Dirk Meyer, 1931

Dirk Meyer to Job Breuklyn, 1933

Breuklyn to Eunice Earley, 1934

Eunice Earley to Eunice Earley Trust, 1969

Harry noted, "Boy, no one held onto it very long. That
makes sense, remember we read that people kept getting
rid of it, probably due to the haunting."

"I don't see anything about the rights of the
Lightfoots?" Sue puzzled over the papers. Harry took out
a pile of books from his pack, and opened the history,
Getting Rich on the Old Post Road.

"I read in here that the library was a tavern at one time,
and was used as a jail, too. That's because in olden times,

jails were just holding places for people until trial, and they would stay in a cellar or barred room just anywhere, and had to pay for their food. Unless they were poor of course, and then they relied on begging the mercy of townspeople to bring them food. But other than being awful, jails weren't used for punishment; a guilty person was physically punished, with branding, people throwing things at them, or worse.

"The only people who were imprisoned as punishment, were people who owed debts they couldn't pay."

"So you think that's the Black and Dun Inn, then? What about the parchment from the library, that goes way back before this one. Also, there's a big gap from Eunice's ownership, to her Trust. I wish I still had that biography of hers to read now!"

"I happen to have it right here," and Harry pulled out *Smoked* from the bottom of his pile. He looked sheepish. "I pulled it off the shelf that night to take it home to read it; well, really because I was hoping to find the messages from your ghost, in the margins."

Chapter 42

Smoked

Harry was writing and Sue had her nose in the tobacco heiress's biography, when a young woman knocked and entered the conference room.

"Hello, Sue," the woman said as she unloaded a tray and unpacked take-out bags of food. "Your father sent lunch for you and your friend. He'll be in, in a few."

"Thanks, Judy! Meet Harry. Harry, this is Judy, who works with my father's office. How are you, Judy?"

Harry stood and shook hands with Judy and said he was very pleased to know her and would like to work there too, someday. Sue giggled. Judy responded that she was doing well, busy after the summer lull, pleased to meet Harry and hoped both Harry and Sue would return in the future. She excused herself and shut the glass door behind her, just as Sue's father arrived to open it.

"Thanks for lunch, Sir!" Harry popped up and sat down again when Sue's dad waved to the chair and poured himself an iced tea.

"Well! What have we got?" Dad took a look at their piles as the children ate their lunch. "Wow, pretty good work. What do you make of it?"

"Dad. There's nothing about the library here, or about the Lightfoots' rights, or anything. And we think there are probably some deeds missing from this collection."

"Hmm-mm. Well. If we look more closely at the Deed descriptions, usually there is a recitation of some of the title history, to identify that this property is the property received by the owner from so-and-so, and so on. That's how searchers piece together a chain of title.

"As to the Trust, the terms of the Trust document would not be recorded here. Trusts are private; it's just the trust's ownership of the library property which is recorded for the public. It seems Ms. Earley made the trust during her lifetime and transferred the property into the Trust. As I recall from the plaque on the building, the Library itself was dedicated in 1974."

They examined the first deed of those spread on the table, the Black and Dun Inn; it referenced the purchase of the property from a Casper Hendrickson. "We found out that Casper Hendrickson sold a property to Tom Lightfoot in 1780! The library parchment said Cornelis Hendrickson was the one who first bought the property from Sam Lightfoot, for the price of an iron shovel," Sue recalled, as she reviewed her notes.

"And Dad, get this! Harry's research showed that the property changed hands so many times because of suspected haunting.

"And I am reading this Eunice Earley book, right? She was mostly travelling around the world between different properties and the book doesn't indicate anything was happening with this particular property until later in her life. Then she hung out with a woman who claimed to have psychic ability, in the 1960s and '70s. They had their friends to the old Hendricksen/Breuklyn house for a seance, to summon the spirits to communicate with them.

"The ghost of a little girl talked to the psychic woman at the seance. She said her father had rights to the house, but instead he was jailed with his family in a room in the tavern, because he owed money for debts he could not afford to pay. Her father died there, but her mother was afraid to tell anyone because she did not know what would happen to her and their child, the little girl. So the girl's mother just burned him up in the fireplace. The girl's mother died soon after, and the girl did the same with her mother's body, and stayed hidden in their jail room. She figured out secret ways through the house to get things she needed. She never got out, and no one ever came for her, and so she remains. Of course, she died long ago." Sue and Harry stared at each other.

"So anyway, Eunice decided never to live in the house herself, but instead she gave it to the town as a library. And she tried to make it right that it could never be sold if a child descended from them needed to live in the house. And the secret apartments were preserved."

Sue's father whistled. "What a story!"

Harry said, "If it's true, her remains must be there somewhere. We didn't find her bones when we were looking around. Thank goodness."

Sue nodded. "It really is a grave, then."

"All the more reason to respect the place."

"Dad. Can't we file a quiet title case?"

Her father whistled again. "The thing is kids, we can't just file an action. We would need a person in interest. A person who has a claim to the title. Like Mary maybe, if there were evidence that she has some claim; and it's my understanding, from what you've told me, that she has no interest in fighting these dangerous people for a right to live there."

Harry had been listening and thinking. Then he spoke up. "But it sounds like Eunice Earley wanted the place to be a library. And they are trying to close the library to defeat that purpose. Don't we have an interest in keeping our library? Can't we take it to court?"

"Well, that is another way of going at it. We would need to see the terms of the trust, but maybe someone representing the town could ask to see it, and to remove the trustee and substitute another, based on the evidence of bad faith you've stumbled into. Tough proofs...but you two have done a great job digging into and thinking about this!

"Time to pack it in for today, though. It's a beautiful day, you should enjoy the rest of your day off."

"Too bad we can't go to the library," Harry said. "I could use some serious computer time researching more local history online. Do you know, some of the old Native American colonial deeds are actually archived online."

Sue's father pointed to Sue. "Oh, your mom has some good news for you. She spoke with the Director of the County Libraries." Sue groaned. "No, it's good. The library will be open tomorrow." Sue looked stricken.

"No, you don't have to worry, Kaycee is on leave. It will be substitute staff and the Director herself. With extended hours, until they can make up in attendance for the days closed. The Director wants to work with your Freep on planning a Halloween party for everyone, at the library. Think you can do it?"

Harry asked Sue, "What does our ghost writer say?"

Chapter 43

R.I.P.

Angelica pulled up a copy of *The Freep – SPECIAL HALLOWEEN EDITION* on one of the Library computers, for display during the special event. Doreen nudged her off the chair and took the seat, reading the screen.

"The photos look great," she said. There were the pictures throughout, the funny picture of Wanda and the chandelier, captioned, *New Librarian Ms. Wanda?*; the dim figure at the top of the dark stairs, the grease pencil threat on the mirror, the reflections back of their own flashlights.

This special edition details The Freep's investigative report about evidence related to ghosts at the Semblance Public Library. But human evil was uncovered also, as reported here. The Freep's staff writers investigated the haunting events.

We discovered a number of adults acted in a conspiracy to frighten us away from the library. These people were hoping that if the public believed in ghosts at the library, patrons would stay away, the library would not meet its targeted number of visitors, and would close. They hoped to sell the library.

While we were in the library for a midnight investigation, we discovered a threat written on the mirror in the Poetry Room: GO AWAY. DON'T COME BACK HERE. We suspect this threat was written by the people trying to scare us away. We suspect they showed us a ghost in the Club Room using video. We figured out that the voices and smells we detected when no one appeared to be present, were carried from other rooms through the ventilation system. We also found a working fireplace, in the rooms which are sealed off from the library behind walls. For the protection of the library and public users in the future, we have agreed to maintain the secrecy of the means by which we entered those rooms.

We did find rumors of peculiar disturbances throughout the history of the property.

A title search showed that Tom Lightfoot bought the property in 1780, a hundred years after a Lightfoot first gave away the property. Old parcel maps were checked, which show that the Lightfoot deed was, indeed, for the library plot. Lightfoot heirs may still own the property, because there is no record of later transfers by Tom Lightfoot. But proof of Tom's rights must have been lost, hidden or buried, because the same lot was sold by a "Hendrickson" to the Black and Dun Inn.

The property was passed to other people since, over the years, until the famed Eunice Earley trust benefitting the current Library.

We found a possible heir to the library real estate, Mary Lightfoot. With the donated help of a lawyer, Lightfoot filed a court case to "quiet title" in the county court of equity. "Equity" means fairness.

The other party in the case, Trust Agent D'Amico, did not appear in court. Investigation by Mary's lawyers show D'Amico is a target in a criminal investigation against his cousin's construction business, and he had fled from the country.

In court, Mary Lightfoot proposed a solution to the ownership conflict. If she owned the title based on the Tom Lightfoot record, she would deed the property to the town outright so it could remain a library. She thought her ancestors would want the land to remain in common for everyone's use and benefit. The court found Mary Lightfoot's proposal, to give the library to the town, to be a fair way to end the case, and achieves what was intended by the Eunice Earley trust, which was the only other claim on the title.

Librarian Ms. Kaycee has reportedly moved away with her family. The Semblance Library Board and County Library system had no record of any library staff called Wanda, and she has not been seen since to our knowledge.

Now that our library is safe, we hope you will all come often and use this wonderful place! Celebrate with us at the Semblance Public Library Halloween Party, Friday October 28 at 7.

"It really came out great!" Doreen said. "All of it, right?" Sue beamed at Harry, who was staring into a giant jar of black and orange jelly candies, trying to calculate about how many there were inside, for the guessing contest to be held.

A photo booth was set up in front of the fireplace, where Angelica and Jacky were modeling an assortment of Halloween masks for each other. They ended up snapping themselves with heads together making silly and sweet faces of their very own.

Rowan and Mary arrived, and Sue turned and hugged them both. "You look amazing!" They were both in flowing patterned skirts, bright t-shirts and necklaces of stones, with flat spare sandals. They moved together so calmly in steps like a dance; the moving shadows on the floor from their skirts seemed like circles of protected space.

"Hi!" Hanna waved at them from her perch on a stepstool in the hallway, where she was hanging apples on yarn strings of different lengths from the branches of the chandelier. Hanna's uncle had moved away again, but she had got in the habit of spending lots more extra time helping at the library, and she was practically running the place.

People were rushing in now, as the wind had come up and was rattling the windows. With each entry, leaves were tumbling in under the doors like small animals scurrying inside. Their new librarian, Ms. Valentina, carried a big box down the stairs, smiling and winking under her witch's hat when she saw them. "Refreshments for our spooky family movie," and she moved lightly down the hall, weaving between excited children mobbing her.

Sue's parents arrived with Joella and Georgie, and neighbors approached them to chat. Georgie in his superhero mode wriggled his hand free and ran to Sue, followed by Joella who was a black cat tonight. The little group of Freep, friends and siblings grouped themselves just inside the reading room, which was empty now as the herd crowded toward the refreshments in the community room and the games set up in the children's room.

Georgie looked up the stairs curiously, and then asked the rest of them, "Does this mean our ghost friend is gone?"

When a book flew off the top shelf behind them and clunked onto the floor, Jacky screamed.

The End

About June Seas

June Seas has lived her own adventures working as a lawyer, as a teacher and as a children's librarian. She most thoroughly enjoyed her service in an actual historic haunted library with a loving and supportive family community, and the very best kind of library staff. She lives with her family, including her Dog.

Also By

Made in the USA
Monee, IL
19 December 2024

74468530R00146